Making Southern brides beautiful is top priority for hat designer Missy DuBois, but sometimes her Louisiana studio moonlights as a crime-solving headquarters . . .

While driving to her hat shop, Crowning Glory, Missy accidentally sideswipes a car parked in front of Dogwood Manor, an antebellum mansion being converted into a high-end hotel by the much-reviled property developer Herbert Solomon. Of course, the car is his Rolls Royce. But Solomon is too busy berating his contractor and interior designer to worry about a little fender bender. When Missy returns to check out the mansion's chapel where her latest client will be married, she finds the developer dead on his property. After an autopsy finds poison in his body, Missy's shop is then flooded right before it's supposed to be featured in an article about wedding-veil trends. Now before everything becomes sheer disaster, she'll have to train her sights on finding a killer . . .

Books by Sandra Bretting

MURDER AT MORNINGSIDE

SOMETHING FOUL AT SWEETWATER

SOMEONE'S MAD AT THE HATTER

DEATH COMES TO DOGWOOD MANOR

Published by Kensington Publishing Corporation

Death Comes to Dogwood Manor

Sandra Bretting

LYRICAL UNDERGROUND
Kensington Publishing Corp.
www.kensingtonbooks.com

LYRICAL UNDERGROUND BOOKS are published by

Kensington Publishing Corp.
119 West 40th Street
New York, NY 10018

All Kensington titles, imprints, and distributed lines are available at special quantity discounts for bulk purchases for sales promotion, premiums, fundraising, educational, or institutional use.

Special book excerpts or customized printings can also be created to fit specific needs. For details, write or phone the office of the Kensington Sales Manager: Kensington Publishing Corp., 119 West 40th Street, New York, NY 10018. Attn. Sales Department. Phone: 1-800-221-2647.

Lyrical Underground and Lyrical Underground logo Reg. US Pat. & TM Off.

First Electronic Edition: June 2018
eISBN-13: 978-1-5161-0574-8
eISBN-10: 1-5161-0574-5

First Print Edition: June 2018
ISBN-13: 978-1-5161-0577-9
ISBN-10: 1-5161-0577-X

Printed in the United States of America

CHAPTER 1

Kudzu vines hung over the mansion's chain-link fence like tattered green bath mats tossed there to dry. Nothing could obscure what lay behind the overgrown fence, though—a beautiful antebellum mansion left to crumble and fade in the Louisiana sun.

I'd driven by the 1850s showpiece on this Monday morning to see what all the fuss was about. I'd read about the mansion in the real estate section of the *Bleu Bayou Impartial Reporter*, and since my morning commute took me nearby, I'd veered from LA-18 for a peek.

I owned a hat shop in town called Crowning Glory, so I spent my days crafting custom wedding veils, fascinators, and whatnot for brides who got married on the Great River Road. But my nights? Those told a different story. At night, I dreamt about grand Doric columns, scrolled corbels nestled beneath pitched roofs, and elegant staircases that swept toward heaven.

All like the finishing touches on this mansion. Well, maybe not now, since cracks veined the two-story columns, paint flaked from the carved corbels, and even more kudzu covered the marble staircase. But, no matter.

Not even a scaffold on the eastern side could obscure its beauty. The second-story scaffold was new, since it wasn't in the newspaper photo. It looked like a giant Tinkertoy set had been clicked into place under the windows, and workers had erected another set over the front door. A Been There, Dump That trash container, layered with hunks of plaster, clumps of rotted wood, and discarded two-by-fours, held the refuse like an overturned box for the Tinkertoys.

I slowly cruised past the Dumpster on the empty road. The layers of debris stair-stepped to an old whiskey barrel, which caught my eye. The barrel lay on its side and fingers of sunlight reached through the broken staves, like the dying whiskey maker's outstretched hand.

The cask sparked a memory. A similar barrel had appeared about eight months ago, when I arrived for work on New Year's Day to find it in the parking lot behind my hat studio. A trickle of blond, blood-splattered hair spilled from the opening of that one, like dirty salt poured onto black, peppery asphalt. The scene had mesmerized and repelled me at the same time.

Crrraaassshhh!

I immediately hit the brakes and my Volkswagen skidded to a stop. *Sweet mother of pearl!* A cloud of pea gravel and road dust swirled around me. I'd obviously slammed into something...but what?

The only sounds came from the rush of blood whooshing between my ears and tanker trucks that rumbled down nearby LA-18.

And then I heard it. The unmistakable *clunk* of something hard falling on the road behind me.

Reluctantly, I dragged my gaze to the rearview mirror. Sure enough, I'd sideswept a car that was parked under an unusually robust clump of kudzu. The impact sheared the side mirror clean off its base, and the shiny metal orb rolled merrily along Church Street, end over end, as if happy to be free of the car.

And not just any car. I'd struck a Rolls-Royce Silver Shadow, which hulked by the side of the road like a shiny Marathon oil tanker.

Only one person around here could afford such a nice car, and only one person would park it so willy-nilly. Herbert Solomon, one of Louisiana's most notorious billionaires, had to be nearby.

Dagnabit! I'd had the distinct *dis*pleasure of meeting Mr. Solomon when I first moved to Bleu Bayou, more than two years ago now. It'd happened at Morningside Plantation, another grand old home not far from here, when a wedding planner hired me to make a custom veil for a bride.

The bride turned out to be Mr. Solomon's daughter, Trinity. Only, the girl never got to wear her custom veil, because someone murdered her the night before the big event. The crime rocked our little community, and it hardened Mr. Solomon even more, if that was at all possible.

Since then, he'd handled his grief in a most unusual way. While others might turn to exercise classes, support groups, or, unfortunately, copious amounts of alcohol to dull the pain, he chose a different path. He charged through southern Louisiana with his checkbook open and offered to buy any antebellum property an owner cared to sell, for twice its appraised value.

He didn't care about preserving these historic gems. No, his goal was to renovate them into high-end hotels and wedding venues and become the area's first gazillionaire. He didn't always succeed, but it wasn't for a lack of trying.

Apparently, he'd sweet-talked the owners of Dogwood Manor into selling it to him, since his car skulked on the property. *Is nothing sacred? Why do people keep selling to him?* Before long, this stretch of the Mississippi River would become known as "hotel row," and not a historic site like it was meant to be, where gracious antebellum homes paid homage to the best and worst parts in Louisiana's history.

If I didn't feel so guilty about knocking his side mirror clean off its base, I might charge into the mansion and give Mr. Solomon a piece of my mind. Or, as my granddaddy would say, I'd "lay down the country and lay it down good."

Instead, I pulled the Volkswagen to the side of the road and hopped out of the car. Once I slammed Ringo's door shut—I'd nicknamed my car for another, more famous, Beatle—I hightailed it to the mansion.

Heat radiated off the asphalt and warmed the soles of my ballet flats, even at eight in the morning, as I made a beeline for a massive iron gate left to stand between brand-new sections of chain link. A Master padlock held the original gate closed, which meant I'd have to come up with plan B to get inside the property.

I carefully threaded my face between two of the gate's rusty bars and gazed over the lawn.

Tools lay everywhere. A belt sander topped a pile of shutters; two wood sawhorses held what I guessed to be the front door, since a blue plastic tarp covered a hole over the entrance; and an industrial pressure washer suckled at a rusty faucet.

"Yoo-hoo!" While tools lay everywhere, the people who operated them were nowhere to be found. "Anyone here?"

A cicada in a nearby rosebush provided the only response.

I frowned and pulled away from the bars. I could leave a note on the windshield of Mr. Solomon's Rolls and explain what happened. Or I could call his office and confess my mistake, hopefully to an answering machine. Then again, I had a perfectly good Allstate insurance agent back in town who might be willing to bear his tongue-lashing in my place.

But none of those options sounded good. They all sounded cowardly, not to mention downright unneighborly. I paused, and in a moment, the problem resolved itself. Someone's voice rose above the cicada, loud and clear, and his sharp words roiled under the plastic tarp.

"We open in five days. Five days! Do you understand that?" The voice came from inside the mansion, and the speaker didn't wait for a response. "We're running out of time, gentlemen."

There was no mistaking Mr. Solomon's voice. While his tone made me rethink my enthusiasm for a face-to-face meeting, I didn't have much choice at this point, so I took a deep breath and grasped the brand-new padlock on the gate. Whoever placed it there forgot to engage the lock, bless his heart, and the shackle hovered over the locking mechanism. One twist and the gray chain slithered to the ground.

I waited for the last link in the chain to drop. Then I pushed on the massive iron gate for all I was worth.

Cccrrreeeaaakkk! Slowly, it yawned open, like every rusted gate in every low-budget horror movie I'd ever seen. The only things missing were a creepy butler in a tuxedo jacket and the minor chords of Beethoven's *Sonata No. 17.*

Thank goodness I'd opted to wear ballet flats today. I carefully stepped around dropped nails, shards of wood, and broken kudzu vines to reach the marble staircase and the makeshift front door.

The scaffold loomed above me. *Is it bad luck to walk under a scaffold, à la a ladder?* Since I guessed not, I ducked beneath the planks and emerged in a cavernous foyer with whitewashed walls and a stained-glass window at the tippy top. A floating staircase, with mahogany banisters, rose through the center of the foyer and split the house in two. One wing led east, while the other headed west. The scent of sawdust and turpentine tinged the air.

I didn't have much time to look around, though, since the voice returned.

"No excuses, gentlemen! Either meet the damn deadline, or you don't get paid."

As soon as he fell silent, footsteps scurried across the floor, as if Mr. Solomon's audience couldn't wait to escape. Someone quickly popped around the corner, and I nearly toppled back against the tarp.

"Whaddya want?" An older man in an orange vest and battered hard hat appraised me warily.

"Um, hello."

He appeared to be a supervisor, since he held a paint-flecked clipboard.

"I need to speak to Mr. Solomon. Can you tell me where he is?"

"Unfortunately, yes." The foreman rolled his eyes. "He's always hanging around here. We'd finish this project a hell of a lot quicker if he'd just stay away."

"I won't keep you, then. I just need to know where he is."

Little by little, the man's jaw untensed. "Yeah, okay. Sorry about that. Didn't mean to take it out on you. It's just that Mr. Solomon's paying me good money to oversee this project, but he won't let me do my job. The whole crew's ready to mutiny."

"Uh, that's too bad. Could you maybe tell me which way to go?"

He flicked the clipboard east. "He's over there, in the library. I'm warning you, though. You might be sorry you asked for him."

"Fair enough. And I'm sorry about your troubles, Mr...."

"Truitt. It's Shep Truitt. I'm the construction foreman here. Or so I like to think. To hear Mr. Solomon tell it, he's the one doing all the work."

Before the scowl could return, I carefully sidestepped the foreman. Apparently Shep Truitt had plenty to say about his employer, and all day to say it. "Thank you," I called over my shoulder as I hurried away.

After a few steps, I entered the hall to the east wing, which was covered in muslin to protect the hardwood from paint splatters. My feet slapped the runner, like a dry paintbrush hitting the side of a can, and I passed a jumble of paint rollers, tape, and caulk. The walls were primed, but not yet painted, and a raw-wood chair rail ran down the length of it.

By the time I reached a double-wide door at the end of the hall, after passing a half-dozen closed doors on either side, the construction noise resumed. Someone fired up a belt sander on the second floor, while hammers and nail guns took up the chorus. Before long, a symphony of *clanks* and *whirs* and *bangs* rang out.

The double-wide door lay open at the end of the hall. I stepped into the library, which was lined from floor to ceiling with glimmering mahogany bookcases. On each side of the cases sat elaborate end tables decorated with cut-glass lamps. A large ladder—its feet shod in shiny brass wheels—leaned against the bookcase nearest me.

That was where I found Mr. Solomon, standing under the fifth rung, as he gazed at a bare shelf. *Apparently he doesn't care about bad luck and ladders.*

He turned when I approached, no doubt alerted by my footsteps in the hall.

He'd aged since our last meeting. What was left of his gray hair was gone, and purple spots flared across his scalp.

"The hotel isn't open yet." He waved his right hand dismissively. "Come back next week."

"That's not why I'm here." I threw him a half-hearted smile as I entered the room, knowing full well he wouldn't return it. "We've met before, Mr. Solomon. I'm Melissa DuBois. I made the veil for your daughter's wedding."

"I know who you are. You shouldn't be here."

Although I didn't expect a hug, for goodness sakes, would it kill him to be civil? I inched closer. "I thought you might've mistaken me for a tourist."

"This is a construction zone, Miss DuBois. No one's allowed in here without a hard hat."

I glanced at his bald head but withheld my comments. Better to use honey than vinegar with this one. "I only want a minute of your time. I'm afraid there's been a little fender bender."

"What do you mean…a 'fender bender'?"

"I kinda knocked the mirror off your car." My voice faltered. Admitting the mistake was one thing, but his icy stare was quite another.

"I'll be happy to pay for it," I quickly added. "The mirror's still okay. It's just not where it's supposed to be." I laughed, but it sounded as phony at it felt.

"You think this is funny?" He finally moved away from the bookcase and walked over to where I stood. "Apparently you damage my car, then you trespass on my property, and now you have the nerve to laugh about it?"

"No, no." I shook my head. "I'm not laughing about it. And I couldn't drive away without telling you. I fully intend to pay for the damages. I just didn't notice your car when I drove by."

"How could you miss it?" He scoffed, until something worse flickered across his face: doubt. "Wait a minute. You weren't texting, were you? By God, if you were on your cell phone, I'll sic my attorney on you!"

I shook my head even harder. "No, no. That's not it. I swear, I wasn't texting."

"Then why didn't you see my car?"

"I noticed something in your trash bin. It's a long story. I just didn't want you to think I hit your car and took off again."

He stared me down for a moment, until his gaze finally swept to the doorway. "Hank! Get in here."

A middle-aged man appeared. It was Hank Dupre, a local Realtor and my assistant's uncle. Everyone knew Mr. Dupre on account of his loud parties and even louder wardrobe. Today he wore an orange polo with red flames that licked across the front panel like wildfire.

"Hello, Mr. Dupre." I realized my mistake right away. "I mean, uh, Hank." I always forgot to call him by his first name, which drove him to distraction.

"That's better. Hello, Missy."

"What brings you out here this morning?"

"I handled the sale for this place," he said. "And I wanted to meet the interior designer today. She's supposed to be a real whiz."

I hadn't spoken to Hank Dupre since Ambrose and I discovered a dead body at a mansion not far from here, which happened at the start of the new year. That was the case that involved a whiskey barrel, which got me into this mess in the first place. "It's good to see you again."

"You, too." Hank turned to Mr. Solomon. "Is that the designer in the hall?" He jerked his thumb back to indicate a petite woman standing behind him. She wore a beige linen pantsuit and sky-high stilettos. The shoes seemed a little unsafe for a construction zone, if you asked me, but she stood barely five feet tall, so maybe she needed every inch she could get.

"That's her," Mr. Solomon said. "Erika, come over here."

The woman quickly approached us when he called, then she extended her right hand. She held a clear Lucite clipboard in the other one. "Hello. I'm Erika Daniels."

"Melissa DuBois. Pleased to meet you." I returned her handshake, surprised by the strength of the woman's grip. And, unlike me, she wore a white hard hat over her hair.

I waited for her to shake Hank's hand before I spoke again. "I hear you're an interior designer."

"Yes. I got my degree at the New York School of Interior Design. I focus on old homes, like this one." She turned to Mr. Solomon. "By the way, the west wing is shaping up nicely, so now it's time to work on this wing. I think—"

"We need to talk about that." Mr. Solomon obviously couldn't wait to regain control of the conversation. "I thought you promised that the library would be done by now. We have our first wedding on Saturday, remember? I don't want you to slap it together at the last minute."

Her smile thinned. "I don't intend to 'slap anything together'. The books will be delivered this afternoon. All the classics, like you wanted. And, I found the perfect mirror for the hall bathroom. I just need your signature on the purchase order."

Mr. Solomon snatched the clipboard from her. Purple spots covered his wrist, too, and I wondered whether the stress of the renovation had caused the rash to spread.

"All right." He removed a pen from the hinge and hastily scrawled his name. "Here you go." He thrust the clipboard back at her. "Hope this purchase doesn't break our budget, like some of your other ones."

"Of course not. Well, it was nice to meet you two." She began to back away from us, as if she didn't trust Mr. Solomon enough to turn her back on him.

"As for you," Mr. Solomon returned his attention to Hank, "I need you to go outside with Miss DuBois and check on my car. Apparently she barreled into my side mirror."

"Not sure *I* can do anything about that," Hank said.

"I need you to take some pictures with your phone and then send them to my assistant." He shook his head, as if the answer should've been obvious. "And you'll need to get the number for Miss DuBois's insurance policy and a photocopy of her driver's license."

"Is that all?"

I detected some sarcasm from Hank, but Mr. Solomon didn't seem to notice.

"I think so. Send those things to my assistant so we can get this sorted out. That'll do for now." Another dismissive wave of his hand.

The Realtor and I turned to leave, an awkward silence falling between us. I finally broke it when we reached the hall.

"I can take that picture for you," I said. "No need for you to run around and do his errands."

"Nah, that's okay. I was on my way out anyway." He gingerly took my elbow and led me to the foyer, where we sidestepped paint cans and packs of roller brushes. "We'll make this quick. I'm sure we both need to get back to work."

"I know I do." I checked my watch. "I have a bride coming in at nine, and it's close to that now."

After we took a few more steps, I paused. "Does he always talk to you like that?"

"He talks to *everyone* like that." He shrugged. "What're you gonna do? I only stopped by today to meet the designer and see the renovations. You know this place is supposed to open on Saturday, right?"

"So I heard. His construction foreman was fit to be tied."

"It helps that Herbert dangles cash in front of everyone." When Hank drew the plastic tarp aside, sunlight leaked into the foyer. "I heard he's paying the workers double time to have the place ready for the wedding."

We picked our way down the marble staircase and landed at the gate, where I rechecked my watch. *Already 8:50. Time to hustle.*

"The mirror's over there." I pointed to an aluminum orb still sitting on Church Street, untouched, since I'd forgotten to pick it up and move it safely out of the way. *Praise God for good drivers and empty roads.*

I stepped onto the asphalt, but that was as far as I got. A scream pierced the air, and it sounded more animal than human.

CHAPTER 2

I turned to see several construction workers run out of the mansion with their hammers, while another one threw his trowel to the ground before shimmying off of the second-floor scaffold. I began to sprint toward the property, with Hank on my heels.

The yowl came from a pickup parked next to the house. A Chevy Silverado, to be exact, with a broken hitch and its tailgate lowered. I headed for a group of construction workers who'd gathered around, their gaze trained on a man who writhed on the truck bed.

Shep Truitt clutched his hand to his chest, a broken corbel nearby.

"Someone help him!" Mr. Solomon's voice boomed through the chaos. "Now!"

I glanced at a construction worker beside me. "What happened?"

"He was trying to load a corbel into his truck, but it fell onto him. Those things have to weigh fifty pounds."

Several Good Samaritans scrambled up the tailgate and moved the corbel even farther from Shep's hand.

He grimaced as he cupped his lifeless fingers. "I'm sorry," he said, to no one in particular. "The thing slipped. I thought I had a better hold on it."

"Well, don't move your hand." Mr. Solomon approached the truck and pointed to a ponytailed worker nearby. "You, there. Drive Mr. Truitt to the emergency room."

"Right away, sir." The onlooker, who seemed to be about my age—in his early thirties—immediately turned and headed for a Ford dually parked nearby. He hopped into the cab and fired up his truck, while others helped Mr. Truitt lumber over to the waiting vehicle.

While they worked, my gaze returned to the Chevy. The base of the wood corbel, which was carved with the intricate design of a dogwood blossom, had been dented in the fall. Bits of wood dusted the truck bed underneath it.

"That's too bad." I looked up to see Hank, who stood next to me. "I wonder if that thing broke Mr. Truitt's fingers?"

"No doubt. Well, at least he's on his way to the emergency room." He gently took my arm again, like he'd done earlier in the hall. "Why don't we take those pictures and get outta here? They don't need us hanging around."

We slowly walked back to the Rolls, where Hank snapped half a dozen pictures of the damage with his cell phone. I promised to e-mail him my insurance information, then I headed for my car.

I drove away from the mansion with Hank in my rearview mirror. *Such a strange turn of events.* Already I'd visited Dogwood Manor, spoken with both Herbert Solomon and Hank Dupre, and, to top it off, witnessed the aftermath of a construction accident. *Ambrose will never believe this.*

I wiggled my cell phone free of my pants pocket, then punched a number on the speed dial. Ambrose Jackson, my beau and longtime friend, always said I had a knack for finding trouble. While I hated to admit it, he could be right.

Ever since I'd moved to Bleu Bayou, trouble seemed to follow me around like an angry rain cloud. It began with the murder at Morningside Plantation, and it only got worse when Ambrose and I found a body in the garden shed at the old Sweetwater place. That was followed by the incident with the whiskey barrel on New Year's Day.

Whenever I called Ambrose from the road now, he sounded hesitant, as if he was waiting for another shoe to drop. But at least he still took my calls.

His voice came on the line after three rings. "Hey, darlin'. Everything okay?"

Smooth jazz played in the background, which meant Bo was working on one of his creations. While I made custom veils and hats for wedding parties, my boyfriend designed couture wedding dresses for extravagant brides. People used to snicker at his occupation, since "real" men don't make ball gowns, but they changed their tune when they learned that people paid $10,000 and up for one of Bo's creations. Like I always said, nothing silences the naysayers like success.

"You're not going to believe the morning I've had."

Once I gave him a rundown on my mishap at Dogwood Manor, my conversations with Herbert Solomon and Hank Dupre, and then the accident in the truck bed, I got around to the real reason for my call.

"Listen...I'm afraid I'm going to be a few minutes late for my nine o'clock appointment. Could you please go next door and let my client into the studio? I don't want her to melt in the parking lot before I get there."

Normally I'd have my assistant, Beatrice, handle the chore, but I'd given her the morning off, since she'd sacrificed her Saturday night to help a bride with a last-minute veil crisis.

"No problem." He sounded relieved that I wasn't asking for more. "Whom am I looking for?"

"Stormie Lanai, the reporter from KATZ."

He whistled under his breath. "Thought you'd be done with her by now. We finished her wedding gown months ago."

Unfortunately, Stormie and I had a history together. She tried to ambush me in the parking lot behind my studio back when Charlotte Devereaux was murdered. She thought she could earn an easy Emmy by getting *me* to confess to the crime. While that didn't work, since I had an airtight alibi for that morning—not to mention a friend who worked as a detective on the Louisiana State police force—she tried anyway, which put her on my "bad" list forevermore.

Since then, I'd handled Stormie with kid gloves. I tried to beg off when she asked me to design her wedding veil, but she wouldn't take no for an answer. Today was the last fitting, and then I finally could say good-bye to her and her ilk.

"She's coming in for a final fitting," I said. "Could you make sure she doesn't have a hissy fit when I'm not there?"

"No problem. And take your time. I don't want you to get in an accident because you're driving too fast."

"Yes, Bo." I tried to sound exasperated, but couldn't quite pull it off. Truth be told, it tickled me pink whenever Ambrose worried about my welfare. Although we'd only been dating a few months, I already knew what kind of wedding veil *I* wanted when the time came. It couldn't hurt a girl to plan ahead, now, could it?

I arrived at the studio a few minutes later, after first passing sugarcane fields and then one of my favorite local restaurants—Miss Odilia's Southern Eatery. By the time I drove onto the asphalt lot at the Factory, which was the nickname all the studio owners used for the building, almost every spot in the lot was taken.

After a few turns around and around, I snagged an overlooked spot in the last row and hopped out of the car. Humidity enveloped me like a wet blanket and plastered my auburn hair to the back of my neck.

I forced a smile on my face anyway and barreled into Crowning Glory. The fake smile lasted exactly two seconds, until I realized Stormie had cornered Ambrose behind the counter, where she stroked his arm as if she was petting a Persian cat.

"Look...Missy's here!" Ambrose yelped the greeting.

"Yeah. Sorry I'm late." Hard to say whether I felt more irritated or amused by her clumsy attempt to flirt with him. Stormie Lanai might have a glamorous job, but she also wore pancake makeup in broad daylight and favored false eyelashes that looked like two butterflies in flight whenever she blinked. People only tolerated her because she was a news reporter for KATZ.

"Ambrose here was entertaining me." Stormie practically purred the words, but at least she released his arm. "You're late. I thought we had an appointment at nine." She slumped onto a nearby bar stool and retracted her claws.

"We did, I mean, we do." I glanced at Ambrose. "And I'm sure Mr. Jackson here needs to get back to work. Thanks for helping me, Bo."

"Yeah. No problem. Good-bye, Miss Lanai." He passed in a blur as he bolted for the exit.

"See you later!" she called to his retreating back. "Don't be a stranger, now, you hear?"

Once he left the studio, Stormie's syrupy smile disappeared. "I hope you don't always keep your clients waiting, Miss DuBois. It's bad form. I have important things to do, you know."

"I'm sure you do. And again...I'm sorry." I dropped my purse onto the counter and took the stool next to hers. "There was a little incident on the road this morning. But the good news is, I finished your veil over the weekend. I think you're going to be very happy—"

"Here's the deal." Stormie slapped the counter, which made me jump. "I've given a lot of thought to what I want. Rex, he's my fiancé, you know, said I can have anything I want with this wedding."

No doubt. Rex Tibideaux, a burly New Orleans oilman, was at least thirty years older than his bride, not to mention thirty times richer. Everyone suspected Stormie only said yes because the deal included a horse farm *and* a fifty-foot yacht.

"Anything I want," she repeated. "And I've decided my veil is much too short for my wedding dress. It's definitely not grand enough."

I blinked. "'Not grand enough'? I thought you wanted a replica of Princess Diana's veil. That's what I made for you."

"Correction…right now I have a *miniature* version of her veil. My veil is only twelve feet long." Her mouth collapsed into a pout.

Far be it from me to remind her that most wedding veils only ran between three and six feet long, which meant her cathedral-length veil was already grand by any definition. Then again, I'd already used honey instead of vinegar with Herbert Solomon, which had seemed to work, so maybe it'd work with her, too.

"Well, that's true," I said. "But yours is just as beautiful as hers. You have to remember, Princess Diana had a very different wedding venue." *The princess got married in St. Paul's Cathedral, for heaven's sake. That venue could handle a twenty-five-foot veil.*

"Are you saying my wedding isn't going to be as good as hers?" Stormie's lashes went wild at the very thought.

"No, no. Of course not," I lied. "But the aisle at Princess Diana's cathedral was extra big and it could handle both her veil and train. I'm not sure the chapel at Dogwood Manor has enough space for a twenty-five-foot veil."

"Well, I don't care. Rex said I could have anything I want. *Anything.* And I want a veil just like hers." Now Stormie sounded like a three-year-old who wanted ice cream for dinner and couldn't have it.

"Let me look at your veil again." I pulled out my most soothing voice. "Would you like to try it on anyway, since you're here?"

"No, I wouldn't. I want to try it on when it's fixed." With a flounce, Stormie hopped off the bar stool and practically skipped away. "Call me when it's ready," she called over her shoulder as she pranced through the studio. "I'll expect to hear from you in…what? Two, maybe three days?"

I gulped. Realistically, that kind of change could take weeks to pull off. "That's not possible." My voice came out much too soft for its own good. "There's the beading to think about, not to mention the lace trim—"

"Whatever." By now she'd reached the exit, where she did an about-face. "Do whatever it takes to make my veil longer. I'll make it worth your while. Rex doesn't even check my bills anymore."

The minute she stepped outside, I wearily folded my arms on the counter and plopped my head onto the makeshift pillow. *Two, maybe three days?* That was barely enough time to order more fabric, let alone bead the extra yardage. I could never lengthen her veil on such short notice.

Or could I? Slowly, I straightened. Stormie never said I had to attach the beads and lace by hand. Given a little fabric glue, I could add the embellishments onto the extra fabric in a matter of hours, not days.

Not only that, but I happened to have a whole roll of Carrickmacross lace, the same type used for Princess Diana's veil, sitting in my workroom.

I'd planned to use it for another bride, but we had six months to create that girl's veil, which was more than enough time to get another shipment.

I rose from the bar stool and stepped behind the counter, where I'd stashed a sketch pad and charcoal pencil. After opening the pad, I began to draw on a fresh page.

A bit of ruching in the back and the audience will never know. The folds would pillow to the ground and hide the seam.

Inspired now, my hand flew across the page. *That's it.* A bit of ruching here at the waist, a nip and tuck at the feet...

The pencil faltered. *Only one problem.* I'd seen some old footage of Princess Diana's wedding, and the poor girl had had to walk forever to reach the altar. The aisle in her church ran at least four hundred feet, while the one at Dogwood Manor probably topped out at twenty.

A twenty-five-foot veil would never fit. Frowning, I dropped the pencil. Maybe I could fudge on the yardage and give Stormie a little less than twenty-five feet. But how much less? There was only one way to find out.

I grabbed my purse and made my way to the exit, where I flipped the OPEN sign to CLOSED. It was time to see the chapel for myself.

Thank goodness my next appointment wasn't due for an hour. That would give me plenty of time to drive to Dogwood Manor, measure the chapel's aisle, and then return with the answer in hand.

By the time I drove down the highway and pulled up to the mansion, Mr. Solomon's car still sat under a clump of kudzu. I quickly parked my Volkswagen and walked up to the gate. Once inside the property, I passed the rosebush with its noisy cicada and skirted under the plastic tarp. A symphony of *clank*s, *whir*s, and *bang*s echoed through the walls and made the light fixtures tremble.

Mr. Solomon would never hear me above the noise. Since I couldn't yell for him, I'd have to hunt him down to get his permission to measure the chapel. Heaven forbid he find me there by accident and wonder why I snuck onto the property—without a hard hat, no less—for the second time in one morning.

Maybe I should check the library first, since that was where I'd found him last time. So I entered the east hall and made my way across the tarp. I had a clear shot to the double-wide doors at the end of it.

One closed door after another passed in a blur. I did my best to ignore the other rooms, although my fingers itched to turn a doorknob or two. There was no telling what secrets lay on the other side of those closed doors.

I hurried before temptation could strike, and then I even worked up a respectable smile to help me sweet-talk Mr. Solomon into letting me measure the chapel. Once I entered the library, though, my grin faltered. No one stood under the ladder this time, and nothing greeted me but a squat cardboard box from Olde Time Books of New Orleans. *Drats.* I quickly retraced my steps and reentered the hall. Mr. Solomon wasn't on this side of the building. Maybe he'd wandered to the other end. *That's it.* No doubt he wanted to check on Erika Daniels's work over there, or, more likely, he wanted to *criticize* her work over there.

I set off again, but this time I noticed something odd after only a few feet. Every other door in front of me, about eleven doors in all, had been closed, except for the first door on my right. That one stood open an inch or two, and weak lamplight spilled onto the drop cloth. Tiny motes of dust swirled prettily through the yellow light before landing on the muslin.

Since I "cain't-never-could," as we said here in the South, resist the lure of an open door, I paused. Although the room probably wasn't an office, given the insufficient light, there was no telling what else it could be. Perhaps it was a storage closet, with cleaning supplies and whatnot, or maybe an electrical room with breaker boxes for the property. Either of those could've lured Mr. Solomon away from the library. My conscience assuaged, I softly pushed the door open.

"Hello?" I carefully entered the room, convinced I might find him there.

Unlike the plaster walls in the foyer and library, this room was covered in wallpaper. Bright green leaves twirled up curlicued vines and ended just shy of some thick crown molding. Even after so many years, the leaves' green color was vibrant.

Above the climbing vines, an antique gasolier hung from the ceiling. The frosted globes cast a pale halo on everything under the light fixture.

I waited for my eyes to adjust to the half light. Then I noticed a boxy object covered in an old bedsheet, which sat against the far wall. *A dresser, maybe?* I stepped forward and waited for the back half of the room to come into focus.

Next to the mysterious object was something left uncovered: a beautiful cherrywood bed, the posts carved in ornate swirls. Under its canopy lay a lumpy mattress covered by an old quilt. The quilt was rumpled and whorled, which meant I'd definitely stumbled across someone's bedroom.

My curiosity piqued, I cautiously approached the bed. A folded newspaper lay on top of the quilt, which I lifted to the light. It was the front page of the *Bleu Bayou Impartial Reporter,* with today's date printed in the upper-righthand corner.

How very strange. I softly put the newspaper down again. Judging by the knots in the bedding, someone had spent the previous night in this room. Their tossing and turning had even jostled a pretty glass finial that hung above the carved headboard.

The finial, which tilted sideways, was swirled with browns and golds, and it reminded me of the old cat's-eye marbles I used to play with as a child.

I reached for the glass ball to straighten it, but I stumbled against a corner of the bed instead and knocked the globe off its base. The finial dropped to the quilt and quickly rolled over the side before I could stop it.

I grimaced and waited for the crack of glass. When nothing sounded, I quickly stepped around the bed. A pile of men's laundry lay on the other side, and the globe wobbled on top of it. *Hallelujah!* The clothes must've broken the finial's fall.

It took a moment or two for the truth to dawn. A pile of fabric had broken the finial's fall, all right, but it wasn't dirty laundry. It was someone's back. A kneeling figure, whose head was tucked close to his chest, and whose feet were painfully askew.

Nothing moved for at least a minute. Not the finial, not the form...and certainly not me. I did, however, finally back away, and then I let loose a scream louder than any electric belt sander or hammer or skill saw I'd yet to hear at the mansion.

CHAPTER 3

After what felt like forever, a stampede of work boots thundered down the hall and into the bedroom.

The next thing I knew, someone grabbed me from behind and yanked me away from the bed. Soon I stood in the hall, which seemed much too bright after the gloom of the bedroom.

"What…what happened?" I asked.

"You're okay now." It was a man's voice, and the stranger continued to grip my shoulders, even though we'd come to a standstill. "Take a deep breath. That's good."

I wrenched out of his grasp and turned. My captor was the ponytailed owner of the Ford dually.

"But who *was* that in there?" I asked.

"Don't worry about it right now. Everything's okay."

"Please tell me. I went in there to…" My voice faltered. *Why did I go in there again?*

Mr. Solomon never said I could wander around the mansion all willy-nilly. In fact, he didn't want me in the house—and especially not without a hard hat.

"Are you breathing?" the stranger asked. "You have to take some deep breaths."

I did as he suggested and inhaled loudly. Slowly, my head cleared and I could think again. "I was looking for Mr. Solomon."

"Well…I think you found him."

"Excuse me?"

He didn't flinch. "You found Mr. Solomon in the bedroom."

"Is he—"

"Yes, he's dead. Someone already called for the coroner."

My knees turned to jelly. The stranger carefully helped me sit on the ground. "I'm sorry you had to be the one to find him."

"Me, too. Wow. I can't believe it."

He pulled off his hard hat and joined me on the floor. "Were you a friend of his?"

"No, but I knew his wife. Ivy Solomon was a great lady." *Poor Ivy.* First, her stepdaughter, Trinity, was murdered at another plantation down the road. *And now this.* "I've got to give her a call."

"That sounds like a good idea." He casually crossed his legs and set his hard hat on top of one of his blue-jeaned knees. "You know, we all thought this was coming."

"Really?" Heaven only knew there was no love lost between Mr. Solomon and me, but I never expected to find him crumpled on the floor of his mansion.

"Yep, the guy was a walking heart attack," he said.

"But you don't know that's how he died. It could've been anything."

"Makes sense, doesn't it?" The stranger slowly straightened his legs again. "He worked day and night, and he lived on junk food. We even had a pool going. I think Randy picked this week for the old man to croak."

A memory slowly worked its way forward. It had happened earlier this morning, when Shep Truitt and I stood in the foyer. He'd said something about the work crew, followed by the word "mutiny."

"Did you guys really have a pool going?" The idea chilled me.

"Of course we did. You saw him. He looked like death warmed over. He only ate stuff he could microwave, like Totino's Pizza Rolls, and Diet Coke." He stuck his hand out. "By the way, I'm Cole. Cole Truitt. Nice to meet you."

"Same. I'm Melissa DuBois." I returned the handshake. "Say, are you related to Shep Truitt, the foreman here? You kinda look like him."

"Yeah, he's my dad."

"I hope his hand is gonna be okay." I swallowed, but a tickle emerged at the back of my throat. "I only came here because of one of my clients," I said, once I swallowed. "I own a hat shop in town called Crowning Glory."

He didn't say anything, which told me he wasn't familiar with the shop.

"Brides hire me to make their veils," I explained. "And I worked with the Solomons once, when Trinity Solomon was engaged."

"Then you understand. Mr. Solomon had a lot of money, but he sure made you earn it. My dad thought it'd be a good experience for me to work on this project. *Pppffftt.*"

The tickle in my throat hardened to a cough. "Excuse me, but I really need some water. Do you know if there's any bottled water around here?" "Sure. I can get you some." He swiftly rose and handed me his hard hat. "Could you hold on to this? I think I saw some bottles in the kitchen. I'll be right back."

Once he disappeared, I set aside the hat and fumbled for the cell in my pocket. It was time to call Lance LaPorte, my childhood friend, at his office in the police station.

I swallowed hard and pushed a button on the cell's speed dial. *He'll never believe I found another body.*

Unfortunately, I'd developed a bad habit of finding murder victims before anyone else did. Although, to my credit, I also had a habit of figuring out who'd killed the victims, which had made Lance eager to work with me.

After two rings, his voice came on the line. "Hiya, Missy. What's up?" Unlike Ambrose, he didn't sound wary of my call. No doubt because detectives got bad news all the time.

"Something's happened, Lance."

"Uh-oh." His tone turned on a dime. "You don't sound good. What's wrong?"

"Are you sitting down?"

"What for? Now, don't tease me. Out with it."

"Give me a second." It was still hard to speak. *Where is Cole with the water bottle?* "Okay. No wisecracks, but I found another body."

The silence was deafening.

"Lance? Did you hear me?"

"Um-hum."

"Is that all you're gonna say?" I couldn't read his mind from ten miles away, no matter how hard I tried.

Finally, he sighed. "You're not going to tell me you're kidding, are you? Just once I'd like to hear you say, 'Haha. Gotcha. It's all a joke.'"

"Now, why would I do that?" My voice rose a level or two, which only made my throat feel worse. "I don't have time to harass you with prank calls."

"A guy can hope, can't he?"

"Did you even listen to what I just said? I found a body, here at Dogwood Manor. It's Mr. Solomon. You know…the billionaire."

"Herbert Solomon?"

I nodded, although he couldn't see me. "The very same."

"Okay, you're not kidding. I get that. What happened?"

I coughed again, but the tickle wouldn't leave. "I came to Dogwood Manor to measure the chapel. I tried to find Mr. Solomon first."

It was hard to believe that Stormie Lanai had sat in my studio not more than half an hour ago, fussing about the length of her wedding veil. We'd both thought it was the most important thing in the world at the time. Little did we know what would happen next. "Anyway, I couldn't find him. On the way out, I kinda wandered into another room."

"What do you mean...you 'wandered into another room'?" While he didn't outright accuse me of anything, his tone was suspicious.

"Okay, I kinda went somewhere I wasn't supposed to go. But let's focus on the important things here. I found Mr. Solomon in an old bedroom. They've already called the coroner."

"Got it. Stay where you are. I'll be right there."

"I knew I could count on you."

"One more thing...wasn't Mr. Solomon an old man?" he asked. "It could've been a heart attack."

Now he sounded like Cole Truitt. "That's what someone else said. But you wouldn't believe how many enemies he had made around here." *About as many enemies as fleas on a stray cat, is what my granddad would have said.* "They even had a pool going on when he'd die."

"Ouch. That's a little cold."

Someone moved next to me, and I glanced up. Cole Truitt silently passed me a sweating bottle of Aquafina.

"I gotta go, Lance. Just hurry up and get here." I clicked off the line and dropped the phone to my lap. Once I twisted off the cap, I took a long swig from the bottle and swallowed. "Thank you," I said to Cole.

"Who were you talking to?"

"Just a friend."

Come to think of it, anyone could've played a role in Mr. Solomon's death. Even a friendly construction worker—like the one who hovered over me now. I quickly slipped the phone back into my pocket. "It was just an old friend from my neighborhood."

"Gotcha. They told me the paramedics are on the way, so it's okay if you want to leave."

"Hmmm." I took another swig of water instead of answering. For some reason, Cole Truitt seemed awfully anxious to be rid of me, as if I didn't belong in the hall. But *I* was the one who'd found Mr. Solomon's body in the first place.

I took another sip and let his comment pass. "I think I'll wait for my friend. He said he'll be here in a few minutes."

"Suit yourself. I'd stay out of the way, though. They're gonna need all the room they can get in this hallway."

Which was true, but it also was beside the point. Only Lance could tell me where I should and shouldn't go, and even *he* had a hard time trying to control me.

Cole didn't budge from his spot. He gave me the strangest feeling, and no amount of water was going to be able to wash it away.

CHAPTER 4

True to his word, Lance arrived at the mansion in under ten minutes. The moment he entered the hall, a stately African American in a crisp navy police uniform, the crowd reverently parted to let him through.

He quickly made his way toward me and offered me his hand.

"Hey there." He pulled me to my feet.

"Hi, Lance."

"We've gotta stop meeting like this, Missy. People are gonna talk."

"Let 'em. I've been accused of worse things."

He led me down the hall to the empty foyer. Once there, he withdrew a notebook from the pocket of his uniform, while I tossed the empty water bottle into a trash can.

I proceeded to tell him every detail about the morning. How I'd tried to find Herbert Solomon in the library...the box from Olde Time Books of New Orleans that sat on the floor...even the way Cole Truitt spoke about his boss' death.

By the time I finished, at least four pages' worth of notes spooled through Lance's notebook. He flipped it closed, then checked his watch. "Is that everything?"

"'Fraid so." I swallowed, annoyed to feel the tickle return. "That's all I can remember anyway. You've got your hands full here, I'm afraid."

"I'll call you later." He gazed over my shoulder. "I need to go inspect the bedroom and establish a chain of command. Don't forget to come over to the station later so I can videotape your statement."

"I know, I know." I didn't mean to sound flippant, but I'd been through the drill many times before. "I'll head over there after my eleven o'clock appointment."

"Sounds good. And you might want to take it easy today." He frowned. "Don't roll your eyes at me... I mean it. Sometimes shock doesn't set in for several hours. And I know how you get. You'll tell everyone you're 'fine,' and then you'll fall apart in private."

He knows me too well. "Okay. I'll take it easy."

"I'll call Ambrose for you, so he knows what's going on."

"Please don't," I said. "We're right in the middle of the wedding season. He's got a thousand things on his mind, and he doesn't need something else to worry about. I promise I'll tell him tonight. Just as soon as I get home."

While Ambrose and I had started out as friends, we were now roommates in a bubblegum-pink cottage that sat on the outskirts of Bleu Bayou.

"Good," Lance said. "He should know what's going on with you."

Once our interview was over, Lance turned and began to walk toward the bedroom. Unlike before, when construction workers gathered in tight clumps to gossip, hard hats in hand, now the hall stood empty.

I turned the other way and left the foyer. It felt surreal to dart under the tarp and emerge in bright sunshine. Everything looked so normal outside the mansion.

Over there was the rosebush, where a lone cicada had serenaded me earlier. Beyond it were the marble steps, which led to an ornate gate with a useless lock that dangled from a length of chain. It felt like days had passed—not just minutes—since I'd arrived on the property, and I was surprised to see the sun wasn't higher in the sky.

Once again, the hammering, sanding, and scraping were silenced, replaced by the *cccrrruuunnnccchhh* of pea gravel under my feet. Once I reached Ringo, I started the car's engine and began to drive down LA-18, my thoughts a million miles away. I barely noticed the sugarcane fields, which looked brown in the summer sun, or my favorite restaurant, Miss Odilia's Southern Eatery.

I only snapped to attention when I entered the parking lot at the Factory and spotted cars crammed cheek by jowl. *It'll take a miracle to find a parking spot this time of the morning.*

Unfortunately, arriving at the Factory at eleven was as bad as getting to work at three. No one would leave until lunch, and then they rushed out en masse, leaving the whole lot wide open.

In between, the stragglers—like me—cruised around and around, until the patron saint of parking blessed us with an empty spot.

This time, the saint heard my prayers on the third go-round, and a gap appeared between a tiny MINI Cooper and a white-paneled van in the last row. No doubt the oversized van, splashed with the colorful logo for Flowers by Dana, had shielded the spot from other drivers.

I breathed my thanks as I pulled into the parking space. Once I threw Ringo's door open, I gingerly stepped onto the asphalt. Heat radiated off the pavement in waves as I barreled across the lot and moved through the door of Crowning Glory.

Beatrice stood behind the cash register. While she should've looked rested after taking the morning off, she looked even more strained than usual.

"Hi, Bea." I longed to blurt out the news of my discovery, but I didn't want to work us both into a panic. Better to give her the news in little dibs and dabs. "It's been a crazy morning, but I came back for our eleven o'clock appointment. Where is she?"

"Thank God you're here!" Beatrice blew out a puff of air, which ruffled her brown bangs. "I was worried about you."

I started toward the counter but became distracted by a feathered fascinator someone had knocked to the ground. I gingerly picked it up and fluffed the smashed hat before I returned it to its spot on a display table that looked surprisingly bare. "What happened to all the other stuff that normally goes here?"

"It's a funny story." Somehow, she did *not* look amused. "And I heard about what happened to you this morning. Everyone's talking about it."

No doubt. "Okay, but first things first. What's been going on around here?"

I gingerly approached the cash register, wary of the changes in both my store and my assistant. While Beatrice normally wore wonderful costume jewelry made with enormous rhinestones, today her ears and neck were bare. The gemstones usually matched her apparel—a man's dress shirt, which she tucked into a pencil skirt, for a fun, funky vibe—but now her shirt billowed over the skirt haphazardly.

"I'm almost afraid to ask," I said. A mound of sparkly jewelry greeted me when I reached the counter. "Let me guess…you got stuck holding a baby this morning, and it didn't go well."

"Bingo." She swept out from behind the counter and wearily plopped onto a bar stool. "We had a second-time bride come in. With her whole gang." She began to rub her bare earlobe, the skin raw and red. "The little tyke yanked off my jewelry, but his mom didn't even notice."

"And he took the hat stands off the table, too?" While it sounded far-fetched, stranger things had happened in our store.

"Oh, no. His sister took those. Did you know those things make excellent weapons? She pretended one was a sword, and then the little angel wouldn't

give it back." Her voice dripped sarcasm. "She even got me in the legs...
more than once. Look." She pointed to a hole in her tights.

"Ouch. Don't worry. I'll pay for those. And what's that spot on your
skirt?"

"Jelly. Blackberry, of course. The darkest kind they make."

I moved to a stool next to hers. "Take it to the dry cleaners and charge
it to the studio. Now...what happened to our eleven o'clock appointment?"

"She called and said she had an emergency, so she had to reschedule.
Something about a problem with her wedding chapel."

"Oh, no." My hand stalled. No doubt the bride had planned to use
Dogwood Manor for her nuptials, and now she'd had to reschedule. There
was no telling how many people Mr. Solomon's death had affected. Or
how many of our clients, although that seemed a bit selfish, given the
circumstances.

"I'll bet you dollars to donuts she booked the wedding chapel at Dogwood
Manor," I said, "and now she has to scramble to find a new place. So, did
you hear that I was the one who found Mr. Solomon's body this morning?"

"That's right!" Her eyes widened. "And here I am babbling on and on
about me and my morning. What happened?"

Although barely thirty minutes had passed, no doubt half of the
population of Bleu Bayou knew by now, and the other half would find out
by lunchtime. News traveled fast in Bleu Bayou, or, as we liked to say, it
traveled at the speed of boredom.

"Mr. Solomon was lying in a back bedroom," I said. "I thought it was
a pile of dirty laundry at first."

"Shut up!" Tired or not, Beatrice found the energy to slap her hand
over her mouth the minute she said that. "I'm sorry...I've gotta stop using
that expression."

"It's okay. I understand why you'd be surprised."

"Stuff like this keeps happening to you. I mean...what are the odds
you'd be the one to find another body?"

"Tell me about it. My friend, the detective, came over right away. He's
going to handle the investigation."

"Wow. Do they know what happened?"

"No, not yet. Everyone thinks it might be a heart attack. But the guy
also had a real talent for making enemies."

"I know all about that, remember? He and my uncle weren't exactly
friends. In fact, they bickered like an old married couple. I never could tell
whether they really hated each other or they just loved to fight."

I shrugged. "Guess your uncle doesn't have to worry about him anymore."

"That's true. But what was it like to find the body?"

"Well, like I said, I didn't know it *was* a body at first." Truth be told, the glass finial had captured my attention, not the person lying under it. All that changed when I realized the bauble was resting on someone's back.

"But I saw Mr. Solomon earlier today, and he didn't look well."

"What do you mean?"

"He had a skin rash and he'd gone completely bald." I suddenly realized why Beatrice would want to know. "Wait a minute. Didn't you want to become a pharmacist when you went to LSU?"

While she'd planned to enroll in the pharmacy program at the University of Louisiana at Monroe after her undergraduate studies, Beatrice changed her mind when she realized how much memorization it'd involve. She made the right choice to give up on the pharmacy program, given her quirky personality, but she still was a whiz at medicines and such.

"Let me tell you about his symptoms," I said. "The rash was purple with red bumps. And he didn't have one strand of hair left. He was completely bald."

I could almost hear her mind working. After a moment, she leaned back. "Sounds like a metalloid poisoning."

She must've noticed my blank expression, because she spoke again. "You have your heavy metals, like mercury or lead, and radioactive ones, like radium. Sometimes they build up in the immune system until your body begins to shut down."

"But would that cause a skin rash? It even showed up on the back of his hand." I'd noticed it when he took the pen from Erika Daniels in the library.

"It could cause the rash to spread. We'd call it a *sign* of the poisoning. A *symptom* would be something only he could feel...like sleepiness or confusion."

"I noticed the rash right away." His scalp had seemed bruised when I'd spied him under the ladder. And, although he'd always been skinny, the shoulders of his dress shirt sagged midway to his elbow.

"Well, you'll have to see what the coroner says, but it sounds like he had signs of acute metalloid poisoning." Her diagnosis complete, Beatrice squinted. "Now, the real question is...who would do something like that?"

"I don't know." Although, to be honest, the image of Cole Truitt immediately came to mind. "One construction worker told me the crew members had been taking bets on when the old man would have a heart attack."

"Ouch. That seems a little cold."

"Exactly. And Mr. Solomon barked at everyone this morning. There's no telling how many people he's ticked off along the way."

People like Shep Truitt, as a matter of fact, who had nothing good to say about the man. And if the foreman would confide in me, a total stranger, who knew how much he *really* hated his boss? Ditto for Erika Daniels. While she didn't complain about him, she'd seemed ready to clobber him when he'd criticized her in the library.

"Bottom line is, half the people in Bleu Bayou probably wanted him gone," I said. "And the other half would help them do it."

CHAPTER 5

"Which brings us back to our eleven o'clock appointment." Beatrice glanced at a Timex on her wrist, the only accessory she still wore. "I could always call the bride back and find out whether she can come in later today."

"That'd be great. It'll give me some time to visit Lance at the police station. Do you mind cleaning up the studio a little while I'm gone?"

"Not at all." Beatrice winced. "But I forgot to tell you something else. The little darling from this morning broke our coffee table."

Sweet mother-of-pearl. "And our budget is so tight right now." Even though August normally brought in tons of customers and lots of new orders, it also meant tons of expenses. I normally reconciled the two in September, when I tallied the profits.

"Maybe there's a bright side." Beatrice was doing her best to sound perky. "Didn't you say it was time we redecorated the studio anyway?"

"I suppose." My gaze flew around the room. When I first came to Bleu Bayou, some two and a half years ago, the "shabby chic" look was popular, complete with distressed furniture, flower-print linens, and old-fashioned chandeliers. Now, however, people wanted more classic lines, with clean edges, bold colors, and even a little midcentury-modern furniture thrown in.

"There's no time like the present," Beatrice said.

"Maybe you're right." I tried to ignore the dollar signs floating in front of my eyes. "I didn't plan to do it right now, but this place really could use a face-lift."

Beatrice and I spent a few moments discussing how we'd change the studio if we found any extra money in the budget. After chitchatting for a moment, we were interrupted by the ringing of the studio's telephone, and Beatrice leaned across the counter to answer it.

"Crowning Glory. May I help you?" After listening for a moment, she covered the mouthpiece with her palm. "It's an editor from one of the brides' magazines," she whispered. "He wants to talk to the owner." I motioned for the phone, which she gladly gave me. Magazine writers usually called our shop to get quotes for their stories, but not their editors. I only hoped it wasn't an advertising salesperson in disguise, trying to get me to spend more money I didn't have.

"Hello, this is Melissa DuBois. May I help you?"

"Yes. I'm Peter Kleinfeld, from *Today's Bride.* Are you the owner?"

I quickly flipped through my mental Rolodex. Glossy cover...oversized pages...readership in the thousands. *Today's Bride* was definitely one of the better brides' magazines. "Yes. Yes, I am. How can I help you?"

"We're doing a feature on bridal trends. Everything from food to flowers and wedding clothes. Thought I'd give you a call."

"I see." My shoulders relaxed, since he probably just wanted a quote. "There's a lot going on in our industry right now. Do you mind if I ask how you heard about us?"

He chuckled. "Not at all. I found you on the Internet. Either you have a damn good search engine optimization person, or everyone's clicking on your website."

I smiled at Beatrice, although she had no idea what was going on. "That's good to hear. It's not our SEO person, because that's me. So, what can I do for you, Mr. Kleinfeld?"

"Like I said, we're doing a feature on bridal trends. That's where you come in. We'd like to do a sidebar on your shop. Your design background, the hats, the whole shebang. Would you be game for that?"

I almost shrieked "shut up," like Beatrice had done, but stopped myself in the nick of time. "Of course we'd be game for that! We'd be honored. Flattered, even. You can use the photos on our website, and I'd be happy to give you a telephone interview."

He chuckled again. "That's not quite what I had in mind. I'd like to send a writer down to Louisiana, along with one of my best photographers."

"A photographer?" My gaze circled the room again, only this time noticing every crack and scratch and flaw. The broken coffee table, the missing hat stands, even a large scuff mark on the far wall. "To take pictures?"

"Yes, that's what they usually do. How does Wednesday sound?"

"You mean this Wednesday? That's two days from now."

"I know what day it is. Is there a problem?"

I shook my head vigorously, even though he couldn't see me. "No, of course not. Heaven forbid! Wednesday will be fine. Perfect, as a matter of fact."

"Good. That's good." He sounded satisfied. "I'll have my crew there first thing Wednesday morning. Bright and early. Give me a call if anything comes up between now and then."

With that, he hung up. I silently passed the receiver to Beatrice, too astounded to speak.

"What did he want?" Her eyes blazed with curiosity as she returned the phone to its cradle. "What's happening Wednesday?"

"Looks like we're going to have some visitors." I spoke cautiously, since it was better to give her this news in tiny tidbits, too, or I'd work us both into a panic. "That was Peter Kleinfeld. From *Today's Bride.*"

"Shut up!" This time, she didn't bother to cover her mouth or to apologize, for that matter. "I love that magazine!"

"So do I." *First things first.* "But you've got to stop telling me to 'shut up.' You're not supposed to say that to your boss. Consider this your final warning."

She gulped. "Sorry 'bout that. What did the magazine guy want?"

"He's going to send a writer out here. And a photographer."

"Aaaiiieee!" She paused, mid-shriek. "Wait a minute…why aren't you happy? You should be smiling."

She was right, of course. This was one of the best things to have happened to Crowning Glory in ages. A New York brides' magazine—one of the very best—didn't travel fourteen hundred miles for nothing. It would bring national exposure to our studio…whether we were ready for it or not.

"Hey, there." Bo's voice sounded in the doorway, and I immediately turned. "What's all the excitement about?"

He loped through the door to our studio, no doubt summoned by Beatrice's high-pitched squeal. I fully expected to see a pack of yapping hound dogs behind him, lured by the shriek.

"Hi, Bo. Sorry if we're being loud," I said. "We just got some news, and Beatrice is a little excited."

"You'll get excited, too," she said, "when you find out who called."

Bo sidled up to the counter and casually draped his arm around my waist. "I'm already excited. So, who called?"

"*Today's Bride!*" She squealed again, just in case some hounds didn't hear her the first time around.

"That's great!" Bo quickly planted a kiss on my cheek, but he pulled back when I didn't respond. "Whoa. What's wrong? You should be doing a happy dance. Why aren't you?"

"Because," I said, "he wants the crew to come Wednesday. *This* Wednesday. Two days from now. Forty-eight hours—"

"Okay, okay." He turned to Beatrice. "What have you done with your boss? The stranger here obviously doesn't know a good opportunity when she sees one."

"Haha." I swatted his arm away, even though I knew he was teasing. "I *do* want them to come. Just not now."

"Why not?"

"Look at this place!" I gestured wildly around the room. "We're not ready for a photo shoot. The camera will pick up every little flaw."

"It's not *that* bad." Unfortunately, he didn't sound convinced. "Sure, you could use some paint. Maybe replace a floorboard here and there. And the mirror...is that blackberry jelly in the corner?"

I groaned. "You're not being helpful. I know it needs a lot of work. Maybe I should've told him no."

"You couldn't do that." Thankfully, Beatrice had the good sense to lower her voice. "This is a once-in-a-lifetime opportunity. You had to say yes."

"She's right," Bo added. "And we're both going to help you through it. Starting right now. I only came here to invite you to lunch. I heard about Mr. Solomon's death this morning, and I thought you'd want to talk about it."

"My gosh. I completely forgot about that."

Bo hadn't heard my side of the story, what with all the hullabaloo. "But I couldn't possibly leave the shop right now."

"Yes, you could." Beatrice nodded earnestly. "I can watch things while you're gone. Nothing is gonna change in the next half hour."

"See. It's unanimous." Ambrose gently pulled me up from the stool. "And I won't take no for an answer, so you might as well give in now."

I sighed as I rose. "Fine. I can't fight both of you. But let's get it to go so I don't spend too much time away."

"Deal," he said. "We'll visit Miss Odilia's and order some of her fried chicken." Little by little, he'd inched us closer to the door. "Like the lady said...what can happen in the next half hour?"

CHAPTER 6

I reluctantly followed Ambrose out the door of the studio and into the parking lot, which blazed under the summer sun. A few cars passed us as people left the office building in search of lunch.

"Do I at least get to order for myself?" I asked when we finally arrived at his Audi.

"Of course. I'm not a tyrant, you know."

We didn't say much once we pulled onto LA-18 for the drive to Miss Odilia's Southern Eatery. By the time we arrived, cars filled the first two rows in the parking lot, so Ambrose headed for the third aisle, where he found a spot near the end and parked.

The temperature on the dashboard hovered near 90 degrees. I bounded from the car the minute he opened my door, then I walked straightaway to a forest-green awning that shaded the entrance from the sun.

Colorful zinnias bloomed in purple flower boxes nailed to the wall. In addition to being one of the best cooks in southern Louisiana, Odilia LaPorte had two green thumbs. She'd tried to share her knowledge of flowers and plants with me when I was a child, although I'd much rather have careened through the neighborhood on a bright pink Huffy than learn about flora and fauna.

When I made my way inside, I spotted her next to a hostess stand made from an old church pulpit. "Hey there."

She immediately glanced up. "Look what the wind blew in! Come on over here so I can give you a big hug."

When I moved to greet her at the stand, the scent of cooking oil, cinnamon sugar, and fresh batter immediately reached me. "It's sooo good to see you, Mrs. LaPorte."

She pretended to scowl as she pulled away. "You're making me feel old again. I've told you a thousand times to call me Odilia."

"Yes, you have. I do it to Hank Dupre all the time, too, so you're not the only one. I can't help myself…it's how I was raised."

"I get that." She finally noticed Ambrose, who'd joined us at the pulpit. "Hello, Ambrose. Haven't seen you in ages, either."

"I'm afraid we're right in the middle of the wedding season," he said. "We barely have time to breathe, let alone go out to lunch. I practically had to drag Missy here today."

"*Pshaw.*" Odilia waved away his excuse. "She's always been hard to pin down. Even when she was a little thing, we had to trick her into getting off that darn bike so she'd come in for a bite to eat." She glanced over her shoulder. "Have a seat at that table near the front, where we can be close."

I winced. "I wish we could stay. I really do. But I'm afraid we only have a few minutes."

"You don't want to get something to go, do you? That's silly. You need to sit down and enjoy your food. No use upsetting your stomach. Come with me."

While I wanted to follow her more than anything, I felt like a rubber band at this point, being pulled in all directions. Not only that, but the magazine editor's words kept running through my mind: *Your design background, the hats, the whole shebang.*

"I'm afraid I can't stay." I stood my ground, which wasn't easy with Odilia. "Not today."

She paused, and something flickered across her face. "That's right… I forgot about this morning. You're the one who found the dead body. Such a terrible thing. And here I am, bossing you around. Just tell me what you want to eat, and I'll go get it."

"Some of your fried chicken would be great." I quickly checked my watch. "I need to drive to the police station after I eat so Lance can videotape my statement."

"No problem. Hopefully he didn't make you stay in that big ol' house too long once you found the body." She shuddered. "Even the thought of it makes my blood run cold."

"No, he didn't. And you should've seen how Lance handled the crowd. You would've been proud of him."

"I'm always proud of my son. But whatever happened to Mr. Solomon? Did Lance tell you anything about how he died? Now, you know, I can't say the news surprised me."

"Me, either." Finally, Ambrose got a word in edgewise. "Seemed like it was only a matter of time before that guy had a heart attack."

I lowered my voice, although no one else could hear us. "You're not the only one who thinks he had a heart attack, Bo, but I'm not convinced. I'll talk more with Lance, once he gets the ME's report, but I think someone deliberately killed him."

"Well, between you, me and the fence post"—Odilia glanced around before she continued—"he gave people enough ammunition to hate him, that's for sure. He even tricked people around here so he could buy that mansion before anyone else had a chance."

"What do you mean...he 'tricked people'?" I asked. "He bought Morningside Plantation down the road only a few years ago, and no one complained then. Why would this one be any different?"

"Because it *was* different," she said. "This time he went too far. Didn't you hear? Someone else was supposed to buy that place, but he went around the Realtor and offered cash money on the spot, plus a share in his other properties. That's something no one else could offer. He always did play dirty pool."

"'Dirty pool'?" I scrunched my nose. "I didn't know anyone else even wanted Dogwood Manor. The newspaper made it sound like the place was a disaster before he bought it."

"'Disaster'?" She scoffed. "Ha. That's a good one. That mansion was a steal, and Herbert Solomon knew it."

"Sounds like you have the inside scoop." Somehow Ambrose managed to squeeze in a few more words. "What else did you hear, Odilia?"

She leaned in close, clearly warming to the subject. "I'll tell you, but only because you asked. I'm not one to gossip, you know."

"Of course not." I pretended to agree with her, although we both knew the truth. "You'd never gossip, Odilia. We know that. You're just making friendly conversation."

"That's right." Her eyes narrowed. "You see, both Waunzy Boudin and Hank Dupre had dibs on that property. But neither of them got the chance to buy it once Herbert Solomon came calling."

The names tumbled through my mind. Hank Dupre made perfect sense. As a Realtor, he had several clients who might want to buy an unrenovated property and then make it their own. He'd even purchased an old mansion for himself—the Sweetwater place—which I'd had the chance to visit on New Year's Day.

"You don't say," I answered vaguely.

Waunzy Boudin was a much different story. The octogenarian headed up the Bleu Bayou Historical Society. She was its administrator and the Society's only paid employee, which ruffled the feathers of several folks in town. It happened right after her husband died, which left her with a mountain of bills and no way to pay them. So the mayor put her on salary and let her run the Historical Society. He even let her add a back bedroom to her house for renters, which was against our deed restrictions.

"I do say," Odilia responded.

"Did Waunzy want to buy it for the Historical Society?"

"Not the Society." Odilia shook her head. "For herself. She told people she wanted to retire there."

"But that doesn't make sense." While Waunzy tried to keep up appearances, there was no denying her dire straits. Especially when an extra satellite dish popped up on the back of her home, courtesy of the new tenant. How could she afford a full-blown mansion when she couldn't even manage the mortgage on a Craftsman cottage?

Ambrose finally broke rank and leaned away. "We could stay here all day to talk about this. But I promised to get Missy back to her studio."

"Of course." Odilia suddenly became mindful of her surroundings. She leaned over the hostess stand and pulled out a few paper sacks. "And here I am, jabbering away. You should've said something earlier. I'll get you that to-go order." She motioned to an empty table as she walked toward the kitchen. "You two can sit there while you wait."

"Thank you." I took the nearest chair and settled into it wearily. "I'm bushed. This day isn't half over, and already I feel like something that's been rode hard and put away wet."

Ambrose sat next to me. "You know, I never did hear about what happened to you this morning. People said you found the body, but that was it."

"There's not much else to tell. It happened right after I went back to measure the chapel at Dogwood Manor. By the way, you're not going to believe what Stormie Lanai wants."

He shot me a sideways glance, which made me reconsider. "Okay, maybe *you* will believe it. She wants me to make her veil twice as long."

"You're kidding. That will never fit in a small wedding chapel."

"I know...but try telling that to Stormie. She acted like it was my fault that she can't have an exact replica of Princess Diana's wedding veil."

Ambrose rolled his eyes. "Princess Diana? That Stormie's a piece of work. I hope you told her no."

"Not exactly." Come to think of it, everything that happened afterward could've been avoided if I'd only refused her request. Then I never would've driven to the mansion pell-mell and found Herbert Solomon doubled over on the floor. "I panicked and said I'd try to make it longer. So I went back to the mansion to measure the aisle, and that's when I found Mr. Solomon in one of the bedrooms."

"Was he already dead?"

"I think so. He wasn't moving. I called Lance, and that's where my story ends."

Someone rushed past our table just then, and his side brushed my shoulder. The stranger stopped and turned when he realized his faux pas.

"Sorry 'bout that."

It was Shep Truitt, the construction foreman at Dogwood Manor. My gaze immediately flew to his injured hand, which wore an Ace bandage that stretched from fingertip to wrist. "Hello, Mr. Truitt."

He wiggled the injured fingers in greeting. While I'd expected to see a full-blown cast, the bandage barely gripped his wrist and the silver clasp hung by a thread.

"Hello," he said. "Nice to see you again."

"Ambrose, this is Shep Truitt." I indicated the foreman. "He's overseeing the job at Dogwood Manor. We met this morning."

"Nice to meet you." Ambrose extended his hand.

"Sorry. Can't." Shep nodded at the bandage. "Got a bum hand. But it's nice to meet you, too."

"Looks like they fixed you up at the ER," I said. "I was afraid you'd broken your fingers. That corbel looked awfully heavy."

"It was, but the doctor said I just bruised it really bad. Should be able to go back to work in a day or two."

"Work?" I quickly glanced at Ambrose. *Surely this man knows.* "People are still working at Dogwood Manor? I thought the police roped it off with crime-scene tape."

"Tape? Now, why would they do that?" He paused to consider something. "Although…I thought some of the guys would try to reach me when I was in the ER, since they always have a million questions. But not this time." He shrugged. "Maybe I trained 'em better than I thought."

"Mr. Truitt…didn't anyone tell you what happened this morning?" By now the truth was painfully obvious. "Mr. Solomon died at the mansion." I spoke slowly to soften the blow. "I found him this morning after you left. He was in one of the bedrooms by the library."

Slowly but surely, the man's face fell as the truth set in. "I'll be damned," he whispered. "Why…why didn't anyone call me?"

I glanced helplessly at Ambrose. *Why, indeed?* His son should've called him, at the very least, if no one else had the heart to do it. "I don't know what to tell you. Maybe your crew was so busy calling the ambulance, they didn't have time to reach you at the ER."

"Sure, that's it," Ambrose said, doing his best to be helpful. "They probably panicked after Missy here found the body. I'm sure one of them would've called you this afternoon."

"You think?" Wonder tinged his voice. "Can't believe the old man's gone."

"I'm sorry, Mr. Truitt. There was nothing anyone could do. Your son helped me out afterward, which I really appreciated. I know it's a huge shock."

He shuddered, and his whole body shook. "I should get back there. The guys need to know someone's in charge. Yeah, that's it. I need to let them know they're gonna be okay. Thank you for...for letting me know. Mighty kind of you."

"Kind?" I shot Ambrose another look. "Are you sure you're okay, Mr. Truitt?"

"Sure. Sure I am. Why wouldn't I be?"

With that, he turned and stumbled away from our table. The *clomp* of his work boots on the carpet softened as he rounded a corner and moved into the foyer.

Before I could say a word, Odilia appeared at our table with two lunch sacks. "Here you go. My chef made some extra chicken, and I threw in a little surprise, even though y'all didn't ask for it. What's wrong? You two look like you've seen a ghost."

"Huh?" I said. "Nothing. Nothing's wrong. We were just chatting with someone." I glanced at the two sacks. "How much do we owe you?"

"Now, you know your money's no good here. I've told you *that* a thousand times, too."

"It's very nice of you." Ambrose took the sacks from her and rose. "Missy and I better get back to our studios. I'd love to repay you sometime for the food. Stop by my studio and I'll alter anything you want."

"Might just take you up on that," she said. "So good to see y'all again."

"You, too," I murmured. For some reason, everything seemed a little off-kilter as I followed Ambrose's lead and rose from the chair. As if something had shifted during our conversation with Shep Truitt, but no one had bothered to fix it again. I couldn't quite put my finger on it, and that was what troubled me most of all.

CHAPTER 7

By the time Ambrose and I returned to the Factory, the parking lot had thinned. The lunch hour was in full swing, and only a few die-hard shopkeepers remained at work.

Ambrose chose a parking spot in the second row, where he pulled into a space before leaning across the console and handing me a paper sack. "Do you want to eat this together before we jump back into work?"

"I'd love to," I said. "But I'll probably eat at my drafting table while I go over some bills. Rain check?"

"Of course." He leaned over to kiss me, then he hopped out of the car to open the passenger door. "Call me if you need any help this afternoon at the police station."

"Will do." I carefully rose from the seat. When he leaned over to kiss me again, my knees once more weakened, but I resisted temptation and took a step back. "I think I'll grab some sweet tea from the lobby to go with this chicken. Do you want some?"

"Nah. I'm good. See you later. And don't work too hard."

I waved good-bye and then hopscotched across the steamy pavement, while he closed the car door and headed in the opposite direction. One glance back and I'd be a goner, so I stared straight ahead as I plowed toward the building's lobby.

My studio sat just off the parking lot, like Ambrose's, but the lobby held a secret weapon, a side table anchored by an enormous jug of sweet tea. It'd been called the "house wine of the South," and I couldn't agree more, since we all gathered around the cylinder of brown liquid like moths to a flame. It was the one place we studio owners could exchange gossip, trade war stories, and engage in whatnot.

Although I didn't have time for chitchat today, at least a cupful of sweet tea seemed to be in order.

I entered the lobby and found someone else had the same idea. It was Erika Daniels, the interior designer over at Dogwood Manor. She stood by a fiscus plant placed next to the side table and, for some reason, she seemed even shorter now, since her head barely cleared the top of the spindly plant. That was when I noticed a pair of high heels in her right hand. She'd threaded her fingers through the skinny straps.

She couldn't quite work the tea ewer with one hand while she juggled a cell phone and strappy shoes in the other, so the Styrofoam cup she'd placed under the faucet was bone dry. *Bless her heart.*

"Need any help with that?" Even though I carried a lunch sack, I could maneuver it around to help her with the ewer.

"Do you mind?" She shot me a grateful smile. "I almost broke my ankle with these stupid shoes, and now I have to lug them around."

"Not at all." I walked over to the table and helped her work the spigot. When tea filled the cup, I leaned away again. "I wondered about you this morning. I thought it was awfully brave of you to wear Jimmy Choos to a construction site."

She winced. "Not brave, desperate. All my business books say tall people get more respect at a job site. Plus, these ridiculous shoes cost me four hundred dollars."

"Ouch." I pulled another cup from the stack and waited for her to remove her tea before I put mine in its place. "Sometimes it's more painful to let them wither away in a closet."

"Amen to that. Though, I'm sure I looked like a total dork this morning. I could barely walk straight. You're Melissa, right?"

"Yep. Call me Missy." I returned her smile, since shaking hands was out of the question. "Nice to see you again." In no time at all, sweet tea filled my cup, too, so I pulled it away from the dispenser.

"Likewise," she said. "I didn't know you worked here. What kind of studio do you own?"

"I'm a milliner. I make hats and veils for bridal parties. It's called Crowning Glory. Ever heard of it?"

"You bet. I looove your displays."

"Thanks." A twinge of guilt fluttered through my chest then, since I'd left Beatrice to rearrange the displays all by herself while I galivanted here, there, and everywhere else. "Speaking of which…I should probably get back to work. We have a lot going on right now."

"I understand." She eyed her cup wistfully. "Too bad we can't spike this tea with something stronger. What a horrible morning we've had."

"You can say that again." It sounded like she knew all about Herbert Solomon's death, unlike Shep Truitt, who had to be told the news.

"I heard you were the one who found the body this morning. That must've been awful."

"It was." I paused to sip from my cup. *Nice and sugary, and, hopefully, full of caffeine.* I quickly swallowed once I had a chance to savor the sweetness. "'Course, I didn't really know it was him at the time. I only found out afterward."

"Did the EMS crew get there right away?"

"Pretty much. They called the coroner, too. I got out of there as quickly as I could."

Silence enveloped us as we sipped from our cups. Her thoughts seemed a million miles away as she gazed out the window.

After a moment, she refocused her attention. "This is really a tough break for everyone."

"You mean the family?"

"Yeah, there's that. But for everyone else, too. It's put a lot of people out of work. All the construction guys, the electricians, the plumbers…they all need to find new jobs now. And they're not the only ones. I don't know how I'm going to pay my studio rent this month."

I nodded vaguely. While I wanted to sympathize with her, I also needed to return to work. But that would leave her with only a ficus for company, which seemed a little coldhearted. Maybe I could spare another minute or two to give her a sounding board. "I'm sorry to hear that. Don't you have any other clients right now?"

"No, I'm afraid not. I turned down three other commissions to work on Dogwood Manor. What a mistake. That Herbert Solomon is insane."

"Can't argue with you there." Obviously, she wasn't a fan of Herbert Solomon, either. Then again, how could she be, when he belittled her in front of other people? The way he'd spoken to her this morning had set my teeth on edge and made me wonder how much worse he treated her in private. "You poor thing. I can't imagine having to deal with him day in and day out."

"It wasn't easy, I can tell you that. So, you never had to work for him?"

"Not really. I made a veil for his daughter once, but that was a long time ago. Plus, she had a wedding planner, which gave me a buffer."

"Aren't you the lucky one." She chuckled, but it was bitter. "He acted like I didn't have a brain in my head, like I'd never decorated a room before. But that's not true. I've worked on dozens of properties. I decorated some of the studios around us, and I worked on the governor's mansion, even. She glanced at the second floor. "One of my projects got an award last month from *Architectural Digest*. Want to see pictures?"

"Sure. Why not."

She quickly dropped her shoes to the ground and placed her tea on the side table. Then she scrolled through some pictures on her iPhone until she found what she was looking for. "Here's the studio I did upstairs. It's for a painter who does bridal portraits."

She extended the phone to me. The screen showed a brick-walled loft filled with buttery-white couches and silvered side tables. She'd even stenciled a fleur-de-lis on the ceiling, which was mirrored in a shimmering table below it.

"That's so pretty." My gaze traveled from the table to the ceiling and back again. "You have a great eye for design."

"Thanks. Here's another one." She took back the phone and quickly scrolled to the next photo in the lineup. This one featured a colorful artist's easel placed on a harlequin-patterned rug. She'd copied the black-and-white diamonds in a series of picture frames over the couch.

"Wow. I love the color palette." Reluctantly, I gave the phone back to her. "I wish my studio looked like that."

While she put her phone away, a thought flittered through my mind. "Wait a minute...of course!" I didn't mean to yell, or to startle her, but I must've done both, because she flinched.

"Excuse me?"

I lowered my voice. "Sorry 'bout that. But I just had a great idea."

"What's your idea?"

"*I* could hire you," I said. "I need to have my studio redone, and you now have time for a new client." *It made perfect sense. Unless...*

I gulped. Ambrose always told me my mouth ran faster than my brain sometimes. For all I knew, the girl standing next to me could charge hundreds of dollars an hour for her time, which I couldn't afford. Judging by the pictures on her cell, I wouldn't doubt it. "I don't know if I can pay you what you're worth, though."

"I'll tell you a secret." She patted the pocket where her phone lay. "The artist with the loft repaid me with an oil painting. I sometimes work in trade for people I like."

"You don't say." Hope began to swell in my chest again, despite the sound of Ambrose's warning in my ear. "You don't happen to need a hat any time soon, do you? Maybe there's a big party or a client meeting in your future?" Although the shop's budget was tight right now, the stockroom overflowed with supplies, and I'd happily work nights and weekends to create her a new hat.

"I *do* need a hat." Now it was her turn to look enthused. "I go to the Kentucky Derby every year. I've always wanted to be in *Town & Country* magazine, but my hats were never elaborate enough. Do you think you could make me one?"

"Of course!" There went the volume again. "I used to make Derby hats all the time when I went to Vanderbilt. My clients loved to see themselves in that magazine!"

"Well, this could work out pretty good." This time she didn't look spooked. "Why don't I stop by your place this afternoon and take a look around? My studio is just upstairs, near Pink Cake Boxes. I could come and take some pictures of your place so I know what I have to work with. Will you be there?"

I bit my lip while I considered her offer. I'd promised Lance I'd stop by the police station as soon as I finished lunch. Not to mention, Beatrice was supposed to reschedule our eleven o'clock appointment for later in the afternoon. *Still...*

"Maybe we can work something out," I said. "I have some appointments, but I could give you a call later. I'd love to get you started on this. Now, there's something you should know. The deadline is kinda tight." Which was a massive understatement, but why dampen her enthusiasm at this point?

"A deadline?" Unfortunately, the wary look returned. "What kind of deadline are we talking about?"

"Well, to be honest..."

"Look, it's not a deal breaker," she quickly said. "I'm still up for it. I have time, and I'd really like that Derby hat. But I need to know how many weeks I have."

"Weeks?" My voice faltered, but there was no turning back at this point. "Okay...here's the deal. You only have two days. It needs to be done by Wednesday." I took a deep breath and waited for her to say no.

"Two days? As in, this Wednesday?"

"Yep, two days." My mind went into overdrive again. Apparently I'd have to sweeten the pot to keep her interested. "A bridal magazine is coming to town to take pictures of my studio. A big-time magazine out of New York City." *Come to think of it, maybe I could lay it on even thicker. Give her a great incentive to meet the deadline.* "They're one of the best bridal magazines in the business. Their readership is huge. Huge! I'm sure I could get them to mention you and your work if I asked."

She seemed curious, which was a good sign. "You don't say. How many readers?"

"At least a hundred thousand a month," I said. "Maybe more. Full-color, glossy pages. The photos would no doubt look amazing."

"Hmmm. And you say you only have two days?"

"Yes, but it's not like the studio is bare now. I have some pieces already. Maybe you could repurpose them. Plus, I'd give you free rein to do whatever else you wanted to do inside." I stopped talking long enough for her to catch up. Hopefully, I hadn't overplayed my hand.

After a moment, she grinned. "Okay. Why not? I'll do it."

"That's wonderful!"

"It could be fun," she said. "Like one of those reality TV shows where the contestants have twenty-four hours to make over a house."

"Only you'll have more than twenty-four hours," I reminded her. "You'll have a whole forty-eight hours. And it's only a studio...not a whole house."

"But we have to start this afternoon." She spoke quickly now. "We don't have a minute to spare. Not one minute."

"I agree." I tried to keep my voice in check this time. "So, you can work with that deadline?"

"Look, to be honest...I'm probably crazy. It usually takes two days just to sketch a layout. But it sounds like you need help. And I need the publicity, not to mention a Derby hat. So, yes. If you tell the magazine people who designed your studio, I'll do it for free." She held up her hand. "But you'll need to pay me if I buy any furniture."

"Of course... I understand. No problem." I spoke quickly, too, before either of us could change our minds.

"Great. Call me later this afternoon. I can't wait to get started!" With that, she turned and walked away, her tea all but forgotten on the side table.

My shoulders relaxed the moment she left. What a wonderful coincidence! I'd never expected to run into Erika Daniels, of all people, in the lobby of my own building. Maybe now I had a shot at impressing the writer and photographer with my studio.

My euphoria lasted several seconds before something else flitted through my mind. The memory involved Herbert Solomon, back in the library at Dogwood Manor, when he signed a piece of paper and shoved the clipboard back at Erika. He'd mentioned something or other about her "extravagant purchases," which he warned her not to repeat. He seemed to think she was a spendthrift.

Uh-oh. Am I setting myself up for disaster? Maybe Ambrose was right, after all, and I'd just let my heart rule over my head again. Whether it was true or not, I'd just given a designer I knew nothing about the freedom to remake my beloved studio.

CHAPTER 8

After watching Erika leave the lobby, I headed for the parking lot. A few eager beavers had finished lunch and returned to work early, and their shiny SUVs filled both the first and second rows.

I angled my body parallel to the building once I reached the sidewalk, since it was best to stay in a rectangle of shade provided by a striped awning overhead, rather than melt into a hot puddle on the steamy asphalt.

Once I was within shouting distance of my studio, I spied the CLOSED sign hanging in the front window. I tried the doorknob, which was locked, of course, and then I unlocked the dead bolt before stepping inside. Everything had been put to rights, and the displays looked wonderful again. Even the riding crop nestled among the other equestrian gear on the front table.

Beatrice's handiwork was everywhere. *Bless her heart.* She must've worked straight through her lunch hour to rearrange the displays. I found a hastily scrawled note next to the cash register that confirmed my suspicion. *Did the best I could...be back soon.*

I headed for the workroom without bothering to flip the sign around. Maybe now I finally could enjoy the feast Odilia had prepared for me. I carefully placed the sack on my drafting table and propped some paperwork on the easel.

Then I hungrily dove into the bag. Along with fried chicken, I found a small container of jambalaya, three fluffy butter biscuits, and an equal number of Darigold pats. It didn't take long for oily thumbprints to appear on my paperwork, which my accountant might wonder about come tax time, but the meal was well worth the mess.

Once I finished lunch, I arose with a sigh and headed for the bathroom to wash up. Then I traipsed back through the studio and locked the door behind me. While I yearned to pop my head into Ambrose's studio next door, enough was enough already. It was time to visit Lance at the police station before he sent a squad car out to the Factory to fetch me. That was one scene I wanted to avoid, since the rumor mill already had enough gossip to keep it churning for days.

I hurried through the parking lot, hopped into Ringo, and cranked the AC to high. Thank goodness the police station was only five minutes away, and I immediately found an empty spot next to Lance's car when I arrived.

As always, dead june bugs, dried mud splatters, and streaks of bird excrement covered the hood of his car. One of these days Lance might actually pay a visit to the Sparkle-N-Shine and discover what color paint lay under his car's hood.

I hopped onto the sidewalk, my attention focused on the yucky spectacle. I didn't notice anyone else nearby until a voice called out to me.

"Yoo-hoo!"

I glanced up to see Waunzy Boudin. The stout grandmother strode purposefully down the sidewalk, an enormous purse at her side. Leave it to Waunzy to find a hot pink purse that matched her fuchsia flip-flops.

"Hello, Mrs. Boudin."

She cupped a hand over her eyes to shield them from the sun. "Took me a moment to realize it was you, dear. This gal-darned sun has me blinded."

"No doubt."

When she lowered her arm, the smell of Shalimar perfume reached me.

"How are you, dear?" she asked.

"I'm fine. A little rushed, but that's nothing new."

"Now…that's not what I heard. You don't have to put on airs with me."

"Excuse me?" I asked.

"I heard you had a horrible morning." She reached forward to pat my shoulder, once again conjuring the Oriental smell of cinnamon and cherry blossoms.

"I'll be alright." I kept my voice light to forestall a full-on hug.

"If it's any consolation, it would've happened sooner or later." She leaned even closer. "You know what they say about karma, don't you? What goes around comes around. That's what they say, anyway. Herbert Solomon couldn't treat people like dirt and expect the universe to just sit by and do nothing."

"Sounds like you weren't a fan." Which was an understatement, given the fact that Waunzy had practically hissed his name.

"Heavens, no. Not after the way he treated Hank and me."

"You mean with the real estate?" Odds were good she still had a bad taste in her mouth from the sale of Dogwood Manor.

"That man had no right to cut in line in front of us. He scooped up that property faster than you could say 'boo.' Shame on his momma for not teaching him better manners."

"But at least he tried to restore it, right?" I searched for something, anything, kindly to say about the dearly departed. "Maybe we should give him a little credit for that. No use letting another beautiful mansion fall apart."

"'Restore'? That's not the word I'd use." She *tsk*ed. "I'd call it whitewashing. He erased all of the beautiful details that made that place special to begin with. You know that a British gentleman built the house in the eighteen fifties, don't you? He brought over a boatload of crystal, fabrics, and furniture to fill his grand new mansion. Now, I can't speak for Hank, but I would've kept the house the way it was. It's entirely possible to restore old homes without changing them so drastically. He took way too many liberties, if you ask me."

"But didn't he have to get everything approved by the planning commission? I thought they kept strict guidelines for all the historic properties around here."

"Normally, they do." She lowered her voice. "But don't you know? Herbert Solomon had the planning commission in his back pocket. He could've painted the house orange for all they cared. The last owners never even bothered to request historic status. It's a shame, really. A downright shame."

"I guess. It'll be interesting to see what happens to it now."

"Someone could still go in and fix his mistakes." She seemed to warm up to the topic, and her voice rose again. "First thing I'd do is paint it taupe, like before. Then I'd get rid of those clunky corbels and put up some lacy fretwork. Something nice and airy. Give it character. Who knows how far a few thousand dollars could go?"

"Sounds like you've put a lot of thought into this." While she struck me as a mild-mannered grandmother, the steely glint in Waunzy's eyes told me another story.

"Not really." She tried to dismiss her outburst with a casual wave. "What do I know? What's done is done. Might as well make peace with it. But I really should be going. It's hotter than a billy goat in a pepper patch out here."

With that, she turned and trundled down the sidewalk, leaving a trail of perfume in her wake.

For someone who supposedly had made peace with Herbert Solomon's shenanigans, she sounded awfully impassioned on the subject.

I mulled over our conversation as I continued into the lobby of the police station. After only a few minutes there, my flushed cheeks began to cool and my damp shirt collar dried. That was the thing about government buildings in the South. The minute the temperature outside nudged up a tad, the thermostats inside fell to the sixties. *Shame on me for not remembering to bring a sweater. Serves me right.*

Lance arrived soon afterward and escorted me to the interview room, where I recounted my story—in between shivers—for a video camera mounted to the wall. When the red light on the machine blinked off, he and I discussed the coroner's report, which wouldn't be available for several weeks, and then we talked about the medical examiner's summary, which could arrive days earlier. Lance promised to keep me apprised either way, and I returned to my car and the mud-splattered vehicle next to it.

I vowed to revel in the warmth this time as I fired up Ringo. Even with the short respite at the police station, that vow lasted exactly three seconds, until my cheeks flamed again. I cranked up the AC at the next stoplight and cracked the window open to let the hot air escape.

The driver next to me must've had the same idea, because the car's passenger window slowly unfurled. Unlike mine, though, it didn't stop after an inch, but continued to lower until the driver came into view.

"'Scuse me," a voice called out. "Are y'all from around here?"

I opened my window more to be polite. The speaker was a middle-aged woman with a trendy asymmetrical haircut and pricey-looking sunglasses balanced on her nose. Pretty, she was, in a made-up kind of way.

"Yes, ma'am. I am."

The glasses bobbled when she frowned. "I think I'm lost. Could you tell me how to get back on the highway?"

"No problem. Just stay on this road for another mile and you'll see the on-ramp on your right."

"You'd think they'd put up a sign for it." She sniffed, and the glasses bobbled again. "Guess this town's too dinky to afford one. How do they expect folks not from around here to know where to go?"

"Maybe they figured everyone uses a GPS nowadays."

"Whatever. Thank you anyway." The window slowly ascended, and the shadowy figure disappeared.

Bless her heart. There was no need to insult Bleu Bayou like that. I purposely hung back when the stoplight changed so she and I wouldn't be neck and neck as we both drove down the road.

That was when I noticed the sloped trunk of the car as it flowed through the intersection ahead of me, like liquid silver from a crucible. The car turned out to be a Rolls-Royce, of all things—something as rare around here as the Hope Diamond. *It can't be, can it?*

I changed lanes and drew closer for a better look. The side of the car caught me unawares, and the breath stalled in my lungs.

The driver's-side mirror was gone. Shorn clean off its base, with nothing left but a stub.

What are the odds of two different Rolls-Royces coming to Bleu Bayou... both missing their side mirrors? Slim to none, was what my granddaddy would say.

CHAPTER 9

The drive to work passed in a blur after that. I barely noticed when the saw-toothed outline of the Factory appeared up ahead, since the strange coincidence with the Rolls-Royce haunted my thoughts.

Could the car really belong to Herbert Solomon? If so, who was driving it? I'd never seen the stranger before, and it was obvious she didn't care for Bleu Bayou.

I'd met Ivy Solomon, Herbert's second wife, a year ago, when I worked on Trinity Solomon's bridal veil. She didn't look anything like the middle-aged driver of the car, and she didn't sound like her, either. No, this woman looked younger and flashier, and she wasn't nearly as tactful.

By the time I entered the parking lot at the Factory, my faculties hadn't quite returned, so I mindlessly cruised up one lane and then down the other. As always, cars and vans stood cheek by jowl in the crammed lot.

Just when I was about to throw in the towel and head for the employee parking lot, which, unfortunately, churned chunks of pea gravel and old tar into the undercarriages of unsuspecting cars, a spot miraculously opened up in the last row. I thanked the parking gods for my good fortune and swung Ringo into the space before anyone else could snag it.

Then I hotfooted it across the parking lot until I reached the front row, where the handicapped spots lay. Most of them remained empty, even at peak midafternoon hours, but a brilliant red car hogged the first spot on the right. The Porsche Carrera wore a license plate that read NEWSCHK, which sent my heart into a freefall.

Holy schmolly! Stormie Lanai, the newscaster from KATZ, and my most recent bridezilla, must be nearby. We'd already met once today. *What more can she possibly want?*

I eyed the shiny Porsche warily as I crossed in front of it. Leave it to Stormie to hang a handicapped parking permit in her windshield like a bright blue banner that advertised her total disregard for the law.

I spied the woman through the picture window of my studio before I stepped inside. She perched on a bar stool by the counter, which effectively trapped poor Beatrice behind the cash register.

"I'm back!" I barreled through the French doors, hoping to make a grand entrance that would allow Beatrice to escape.

"There you are." The newscaster spoke without turning, her heels propped on the stool's footrest. "It's about time."

"I'm sorry. Did we have an appointment?" I tilted my head, though I knew full well we hadn't scheduled anything.

"Not exactly." Finally, Stormie spun around. Like before, the pancake makeup washed out her skin and made her butterfly eyelashes seem even blacker. "But I have some news."

"News?" I whooshed up the aisle and tossed my purse on the counter. The closer I drew, the more apparent the lines around her mouth and chin became. She looked like a ventriloquist's puppet up close. "I know we talked about making your veil longer, but I'm afraid you'll have to give me more time if you want that done."

The lashes fluttered once or twice. "That's not why I'm here."

I glanced at Beatrice, who shrugged. Apparently, my assistant didn't know the reason for Stormie's visit, either.

"I'm sorry…did I miss something?" I asked.

Stormie sighed dramatically. "Most folks already know, so I'd thought I'd bring you up to speed. I'm not getting married at Dogwood Manor on Saturday."

"Because of what happened there? I know all about it. You see—"

She held up her hand. "Let me finish. The wedding's still on. Just not there. But we decided we don't want to let anything ruin our beautiful moment."

Beautiful moment? I shot Beatrice another look. Surely a rough-and-tough oilman like Rex Tibideaux wouldn't describe his wedding that way. Stormie must've run all over town to find another wedding venue before her wealthy fiancé could change his mind. "Where are you getting married, then?"

She yanked a brochure from the mouth of her Louis Vuitton satchel. "The Tropicana. That's Las Vegas, you know. They have a lovely outdoor area called the Arbor. Doesn't that sound delicious?" She pointed to a picture of green grass, rattan folding chairs, and towering palm trees. "I got the deluxe package, of course."

"Of course." To be honest, the scene looked rather pretty, with one noticeable exception: A neon sign for the MGM Grand Hotel peeked between the swaying palms. "Would you like to keep your veil the way it is, then?" "That's why I came." She refolded the brochure and returned it to her satchel. "I don't think I'll need a veil after all. I bought a cream Chanel suit off the Internet this afternoon, and the veil's much too formal for that. But, I'm sure you can sell my veil to another bride."

My mouth fell open. "Another bride? But—"

"I don't mind at all. I'll tell you what." She leaned forward. "You can resell it and I won't even ask who the buyer is. Of course, you'll need to refund my deposit first."

She looked so sincere, as if she was doing me a huge favor, for which I should be eternally grateful.

"Deposit?" I struggled to keep my voice even. "I'm afraid it doesn't work that way. You ordered a custom veil. A veil I made just for you."

"And now someone else can enjoy it." She glanced at Beatrice, obviously not satisfied with my answer. "Please tell your boss I'm right."

Beatrice froze, caught between Stormie's breezy nonchalance and my growing frustration.

"I'm afraid you're not listening," I said. This was between the newscaster and me. No need to drag Beatrice into the fray. "Every veil I make is specifically designed to match a bride's gown. Your gown was very detailed, which meant there was a lot of beading on the veil."

I refrained from using the word "expensive" to describe her dress, although the word came to mind. Stormie's Ambrose Jackson original was one of the priciest gowns I'd ever seen, with hundreds of seed pearls and yards of crystal edging. All of which made the design for her veil twice as time-consuming.

"Are you saying I can't have my deposit back?" she asked.

"That's exactly what I'm saying. I've already put a lot of time into your order."

Beatrice softly coughed, no doubt to divert our attention elsewhere. "Why don't we all take a nice, deep breath?" she said. "As a matter of fact...I'll run to the back and grab us some water bottles. Is it just me, or did it get really hot in here?"

She didn't wait for a response. Instead, she scooted out from behind the cash register as quick as a flash, then dashed across the studio. Neither Stormie nor I moved to stop her.

"Let me think about this." Slowly, I sank onto a bar stool as I mulled the predicament. Near as I could recall, Stormie's veil featured three layers of tulle and a crown of Swarovski crystals to separate the first layer, called the blusher, from the rest. The veil featured a straight-edge design, and not a waterfall. "I might have a solution."

Stormie frowned, as if she suspected a trick. "What kind of solution?"

"What if I reworked your veil into something else?"

"Something else? I don't know what you're talking about."

"I could completely transform it into a fascinator. Do you know what that is?"

Stormie cautiously nodded, although I could tell she hadn't a clue.

"It's like the hats people wore to Princess Kate's wedding," I said. "Do you remember that?"

"The little hats! Of course…so that's what you're talking about."

"Exactly." I knew she'd like the reference to the British royal family. "I could rework your veil into one of those 'little hats.' It'd add a whole new layer to the outfit."

She paused to consider it. "Are you sure? The pictures on the Chanel website didn't say anything about adding a hat to the outfit. I don't want to screw this up. You may not know this…but I'm not very good at this whole fashion thingy."

For the first time, Stormie looked insecure, and she trained her gaze on the ground instead of on my face. While she normally came across as a know-it-all, with an easy answer for everything, now she seemed vulnerable and a little imperfect.

Just like the rest of us.

"They probably didn't include a fascinator because they don't sell them," I said. "C'mere. Let me show you what I mean."

I walked over to the front display with the riding crop. In addition to a snazzy silk top hat, the table held a lovely fascinator with a spotted crinoline veil. "What's your suit made of?" I delicately lifted the hat from its stand and brought it over to the three-way mirror.

She frowned. "I don't know how to say it. It's called silk jack…jaq…"

"You pronounce it 'jacquard.'" No need to make her struggle with the word. "And the suit sounds lovely." I waited for her to approach the mirror, and then I softly balanced the fascinator on the side of her head. With a touch of pressure, the comb slid easily through her hair. "We always try to use a different fabric for a hat, so it doesn't look too matchy-matchy with the outfit."

"You could make something like *this* out of my old veil?"

"Absolutely." I gave a confident nod, as she turned this way and that in front of the mirror. "I'd keep the crown with the crystals on it, and then I'd rework the lace into a short blusher."

Slowly but surely a tiny smile emerged. "I could text you a picture of the suit. It's the first time I've ever bought anything from Chanel. I about died at the price, but it's so fancy!"

"Great." I leaned over to remove the fascinator from her head. She didn't even complain when the comb snatched a few strands of hair.

"So, how do you know so much about fashion?" she asked.

I squelched a smile of my own. "It's my job, Stormie. I do this every day. Now, we'll have to work fast. You said you're leaving Saturday?"

"Actually...I'm flying out Friday night. I booked the bridal suite for three nights, and I don't want to miss a moment."

Friday night. My brain went into overdrive. Already it felt like I'd crammed a whole week into one day. It began with Herbert Solomon's death at Dogwood Manor, and it had only gotten worse with the call from the New York magazine editor. The day didn't have enough hours to accomplish everything on tap, and adding one more project just might push me over the edge.

She must've read my thoughts, because Stormie quickly spoke again. "I'll pay you double if you can pull this off."

"Double? But that would be six thousand dollars!" My hand wavered as I removed the hat. "You don't really mean that."

"Oh yes, I do. My fiancé doesn't care how much I spend, remember? He just wants me to be happy."

"Are you sure?"

"Positive." The price didn't even phase her. "Have it ready by Friday night, and I'll pay you another five thousand dollars cash money."

Even her newfound wealth couldn't hide her country roots, and I grinned at her use of the old-fashioned term "cash money."

"That's very generous of you." I searched for a place to lay the hat, and my gaze immediately fell on the broken coffee table.

Think of what all that money could buy! I could give the money to Erika Daniels to outfit my studio with brand-new furniture. Earlier, I'd almost had a conniption fit when she talked about buying some new things, but now she could do it without breaking my bank account.

"I'll do it." My smile lasted a split second, until reality struck. Already my schedule was packed, and the death at Dogwood Manor didn't help matters. But...if I could forego food and sleep for a few days, I might be able to pull this off.

And if I couldn't? I'd be stuck with an oversized decorating bill and one furious bride.

CHAPTER 10

Dawn arrived *waaayyy* too soon the next morning. I lifted my head from the kitchen counter to see that the sky outside had gone from black to pewter to mauve in a matter of minutes.

Scattered around me were supplies for Stormie Lanai's new fascinator, which included white jewelry wire, metal U pins, and some Carrickmacross lace. My eyes watered from having squinted at the lace all night as I applied the miniscule crystals one by one.

"Whoa. Rough night?" Ambrose strode into the kitchen, already dressed in khakis and a pin-striped shirt. The scent of Acqua Di Gio followed him, which was my favorite cologne.

"You can say that again." I took a deep breath. "Guess what happened yesterday? You'll never believe who came to my rescue."

He kissed the top of my head on his way to the Keurig machine. "I give up. Who rescued you?"

"Stormie Lanai, that's who."

"Get out. Not our favorite newscaster?"

"The one and only." I gave an enormous yawn. "She came by the shop yesterday afternoon to cancel her order. She wanted her money back."

"Now, *that* sounds like her." He placed a Saints mug into the mouth of the Keurig. "When did the rescue happen?"

"After she decided *not* to cancel. She gave me the okay to remake her veil into a fascinator. And she's paying me six thousand dollars to do it." I yawned again, sleepy, but satisfied. Even I couldn't believe my good fortune.

"How in the world did you get her to agree to that?"

"It was *her* idea to pay me that much. Of course, it might've helped that I mentioned Princess Kate's wedding. She loves the royals, you know."

"You're brilliant." He returned his attention to his coffee, and that was when his face became serious. "I can tell you were up all night. This coffee machine's bone-dry. I wish you wouldn't do that, Missy. You're gonna ruin your health."

"I know. And I'm sorry about using up all the water. I might've had a cup or two." *Or five, but who's counting?*

"I'm serious...I'm worried about you." He took the water reservoir to the sink and placed it under the faucet to fill it. "Promise me you'll come home this afternoon and take a nap."

"Maybe." I couldn't lie to Ambrose, but I *could* be evasive.

"By the way...why did Stormie want to cancel her veil? She's already paid me for the wedding dress. Did the rich guy get smart and call off the ceremony?"

"No, nothing like that. They're still getting married, only now they're eloping to Vegas. She had to find a new place since the work stopped at Dogwood Manor."

"I forgot about that. I guess no one can use it for a while." He carried the refilled reservoir back to the machine. "Have you heard anything from Detective LaPorte?"

"Not yet. I went to the station yesterday afternoon, after our lunch. I had to give him my statement on videotape. It took forever to get out of there, because we started talking about the coroner's report and whatnot. He might get the medical examiner's summary today. That's about all I know."

"You've got too much going on." He shook his head as he punched the on button. "Anything I can do to help you out? Maybe I can work on some of your invoices or call back clients. You name it."

"That's sweet, but I'm afraid I have to do it all myself." I threw him a grateful—and sleepy—smile. "I'll let you know if I think of anything, though. And I almost forgot...one more thing happened yesterday. I hired an interior designer for the studio."

He whisked away his coffee mug when the machine finished brewing. "We have *got* to talk more often. I had no idea you wanted to redesign your studio."

"I have a magazine photographer coming tomorrow. Remember? And, to tell you the truth, the furniture's kinda outdated."

"Then you should've told me about it," he said. "I would've helped you."

"Thanks, but Erika Daniels is a professional interior designer." Although Bo had excellent taste, he and I didn't always see eye to eye when it came to design. I'd rather argue with a stranger, instead of him, about whether to have scrolled legs or straight ones on my tables and chairs.

"Suit yourself."

I glanced at the kitchen clock. "She's coming to the shop this morning, too. I'd better hustle if I want a few minutes at the studio before the craziness starts."

He blew me a kiss, which I pretended to catch as I turned away from the kitchen.

After heading for the bathroom and a quick shower, I changed out of my Vanderbilt pajama top and slipped on a Lilly Pulitzer shift. The bright pink-and-melon pattern perked me up and made me feel almost human again. Just to be safe, I returned to the bathroom, where I applied a little Maybelline undereye concealer, ringed my eyes with a pretty charcoal liner, and brushed some blush on my cheeks. I also coiled my hair up into a simple French twist, since the day called for a low-fuss, no-muss hairdo.

Once I'd finished in the bathroom, I called out to Ambrose, who didn't answer. By the time I whisked Stormie's supplies into a satchel, left the kitchen, and hopped into Ringo, it was already eight. So I floored the accelerator all the way to the Factory.

After snagging a spot in the third row, I walked to the studio as fast as my tired legs could carry me. The sun warmed the crown of my head, and a light breeze ruffled the shift around my bare legs.

I expected to find the lights doused when I arrived at Crowning Glory, but every light blazed through the front window, including a trio of pendant lights I'd installed above the counter. Since I was usually the first one to arrive, I normally turned on the lights and fired up the coffee machine.

I cautiously opened the French doors and peeked inside the studio. "Hello?"

Erika Daniels stood in the middle of the room, stock-still. She clutched a sequined pillow in one hand and a cut-glass table lamp in the other, her eyes flitting from me to the lamp like she was a wild animal caught in a rifle's crosshairs.

"Erika? How'd you get in here?"

She gulped and nodded toward the workroom. Beatrice must've arrived first and let her into the studio, which was all well and good, but it wasn't what I'd expected.

"You guys are sooo early," I said. "And it looks like you've already found some new things for the studio."

"Just a few." She smiled sheepishly. "I had this stuff lying around, and I thought it might look good in here."

The desk lamp in her hand looked oddly familiar, not to mention expensive. "Is that lamp from Tiffany's?"

"No."

Thank heaven for small favors. "It does look familiar, though. Where've I seen it before?"

"This old thing? I'm going to use it in your sitting area, which I'm moving over there." She pointed to a spot near the entrance. "Under a chandelier. Which they're going to deliver this afternoon, by the way."

"Oookkkaaayyy." She hadn't answered my question. "But I know I've seen that lamp somewhere."

"You probably saw it at Dogwood Manor. It was sitting next to the bookcase in the library."

"That's it!" I said. "Does Detective LaPorte know you took it from the mansion?"

She nodded. "He does now. It belongs to me. I bought it wholesale, and then I invoiced Mr. Solomon for it afterward. Only he never paid me for it."

"Gotcha."

"Or, I should say, his assistant never paid me for it." She placed the lamp on the floor and shook her wrist to work out a kink. "She said she forgot. But don't you think the lamp would look great in here?"

"It *is* beautiful." I walked past her, toward the cash register. "And what do you mean, his assistant 'forgot' to pay you? Settling my debts is the very first thing I do every morning."

"To be honest, I don't think she's that bright." Erika retrieved the lamp from the floor. "Rumor has it he hired his former hairdresser out of Baton Rouge to be his administrative assistant."

"Really?" Somehow Mr. Solomon didn't strike me as the type to hire someone who wasn't qualified for a job. He'd made his wedding planner check me out twelve ways to Sunday before I was hired to make his daughter's veil.

"Hey, Missy." Finally, Beatrice emerged from the workroom with a rolled-up tube of paper in her hand. "When'd you get in?"

"Just a minute ago. I thought I'd be the first one here, but you guys beat me to it."

She waved the paper. "I wanted to get Erika this blueprint for the studio, since she asked for it yesterday."

"Thanks for doing that." I tried to stifle a yawn, but it slipped out anyway.

"Wait a second." Beatrice frowned at me, just like Ambrose had done. "You stayed up all night again, didn't you? Admit it. I bet you worked on Stormie's hat and never went to bed."

"Maybe." I never could lie to Beatrice, either.

"You can't keep this up." She wagged a finger at me in a perfect imitation of my grandmother.

"Yes, ma'am."

"Seriously," she said. "Sooner or later, you're going to crash."

"I vote for later." I plucked the store's calendar from a peg next to the cash register. "It's sweet of you to worry about me, but our schedule is packed today. There's no time to rest." I flipped the calendar open to Tuesday and ran my finger down the page. In addition to working with Erika, I had two clients coming in for fittings, a telephone consultation with a third bride, and a meeting with my favorite vendor. All before 1 p.m. *Welcome to wedding season.* "Do you need me for anything right now, Erika?"

She shook her head. "Not right away. I'm going to double-check the measurements for the floors and walls. You won't even know I'm here."

"Great. I'm heading to the workroom." I took the calendar and started to move across the room. "You guys call me if you need help," I said over my shoulder.

Just then the front door of the studio swished open. In strode Lance LaPorte, wearing his police uniform and carrying a manila folder.

"Good morning. Is Missy around?" He strode over to the counter, obviously unaware of my presence.

There goes my quiet time. While I enjoyed talking to Lance, sometimes our conversations lasted way too long.

"I'm right here." With a sigh, I turned and walked back to the counter. "To what do I owe the pleasure?"

"To this." He held up the folder, which twinkled under the pendant lights. The all-too-familiar logo for the St. James Parish Coroner's Office winked at me.

"I see. Why don't we go back to the workroom and get some coffee?" Odds were good Beatrice had fired up the pot once she let Erika into the studio, which meant we could review the medical examiner's report over something stronger than bottled water.

Beatrice and Erika exchanged quick looks.

"Don't worry, ladies," I said. "We'll be right back there in the workroom." I waved the calendar at Lance to indicate he should follow me. "Give us a holler if you need anything."

I headed for the workroom, Lance on my heels. Once inside, I pointed to a swivel chair by the drafting table, then I closed the door behind him. "You got that report back pretty fast."

He nodded as he slid onto the seat. "It only takes a day or two for the preliminary. The ME worked on Solomon last night."

I sank into a chair next to his. "Here we go again."

"Tell me about it."

Only eight months before, Lance and I had reviewed another autopsy report when the owner of a special events company had died right behind my studio. I helped solve that crime, like I'd done with two previous murders, which established a pattern between us. Lance collected the report from the medical examiner, then gave it a quick perusal. Once finished, he shared the report with me for my opinion.

He balanced the folder on the drafting table, but before he opened the cover, his eyes narrowed. "Are you okay?"

"Sure. Why wouldn't I be?"

"I don't want to sound harsh, but you look kinda rough this morning."

"I love you, too, Lance." I tried to play off his comment, but all the attention on my appearance was getting old. "It's the wedding season. I had a big project last night, and I may have stayed up a little too late." Which was an understatement, but why worry him any more than necessary?

"Whatever you say." He finally flipped open the cover, which doused the twinkle from the foil seal. "Remember what happened with the last case?"

"Unfortunately, yes." Imagine my horror when the police found a bloodied hat stand near Charlotte Devereaux's body. Some of the locals actually suspected me of the crime, even though I had an airtight alibi for that morning.

"At least I'm not a suspect in this case, right?" I shot him a quick look. Although I'd discovered the old man's body yesterday, I didn't know him very well and had no reason to want him dead.

"No, you're not a suspect in this case. Looks like he succumbed to renal failure after long-term exposure to a contaminant."

"I *knew* he didn't have a heart attack." Call it instinct or call it women's intuition, but he'd seemed to have other health problems. Maybe it was the strange skin rash or the sudden baldness that tipped me off.

Lance thumped the folder with his finger. "Someone poisoned him with arsenic. It rose to toxic levels in his blood, liver, and kidneys before shutting down his entire system." He eyed me curiously. "I've gotta say… you don't look surprised."

"I'm not." I leaned back. "One look at him yesterday, and I could tell he was sick. Plus, Beatrice told me he was probably poisoned."

"He never went to the doctor. We already checked with his GP. He probably thought it was something he could just shake off. The ME noticed a strange smell during the autopsy." Lance quickly scanned the page, and his gaze stopped midway through it. "It smelled like almonds. He noted it in the section under 'external investigation.'"

"So...it was arsenic, huh?"

"Yes."

"Did the ME notice anything else?" The words on the page looked blurry from so far away.

"He did. Arsenic victims usually get Mees' lines on their fingernails."

"What's that?"

Lance normally simplified medical terms for me whenever we reviewed a report together.

"It's a white line that appears on the fingernails after someone's been exposed to arsenic. Look here." He pointed to a picture in the folder.

The close-up photo showed a purplish, liver-spotted hand with short fingernails. Mr. Solomon's hand, I presumed. A white band ran across each nail, and several bands striped his thumb and forefinger.

"Okay. I get it." I glanced away, slightly nauseated. "Any idea how long it'd been going on?"

"A long time. Long enough for him to develop hyperkeratosis, too. It thickened his skin and caused raised bumps on places like his scalp."

"I noticed the top of his head, too, when I saw him. Wow. So, someone's been poisoning him all this time."

"Apparently so. The actual report won't be available until next week, but this'll give me something to go on."

At that moment, a soft knock sounded at the door of the workroom.

"Excuse me," Beatrice called out.

"Come on in, Bea." I glanced at Lance, and he closed the report.

"I'm sorry to interrupt." She entered the room. "But there's something Erika needs to show Missy. Will you guys be much longer?"

Lance rose with the folder. "No. We're done here. I'll call you later, Missy. The judge came through with the search warrants last night, so I'm starting on the interviews."

My gaze moved past him to a small table set up against the wall. "Shoot. I forgot to pour you some coffee. Do you want to take a cup with you?"

"Nah. I'm good. And it sounds like you're going to need it more than I am today."

I wanted to protest, but how could I? Odds were good I'd drink half the carafe in the next few hours. "You're right, but don't forget to call. And if I think of anything else from yesterday, I'll let you know."

"Deal."

I followed Lance out of the workroom. Once I stepped into the studio, I spied Erika by a back wall. I stopped midstride and let Lance continue without me.

"'Bye, Lance," I called out as he slipped through the exit.

Once he waved, I moved over to where Erika stood. She gazed at something or other on the ceiling, her eyebrows furrowed.

"Has that always been there?" She pointed to something over our heads. A dark brown stain floated on the white paint, the edges ruffled and watery.

"I'm afraid so," I said. "It happened back in January, when we had those really bad rainstorms."

"Hmmm. It doesn't look good. Not to mention, it could cause mold. We need to cover it up with a primer like Kilz. Then we can repaint it."

I should've remembered to fix the water stain months ago, when it first appeared. *Shame on me for not doing it.* That was the thing about owning a small business. So many projects competed for your attention, and only the most obvious ones actually got it. The rest, like the brown stain on the ceiling, quickly got forgotten. "Will Kilz take care of the mold?"

"Definitely. I know they have it at Homestyle Hardware. We need to do it this morning, so the primer has a chance to dry. I'd run out and get some myself, but I'm right in the middle of finalizing a design for the studio."

I glanced across the room. "I guess I could ask Beatrice." Odds were good my assistant would happily run the errand. Which was all the more reason for me to be grateful she'd arrived at work earlier than normal.

"I forgot something." Erika finally looked away from the ceiling. "Beatrice said to tell you she had to go to the bank. Something about one of your clients finally paying a bill."

My heart sank. Not only had I lost out on my quiet time when Lance had appeared at the studio, but now I had to run an errand to Homestyle Hardware. "Guess I'm the only one left to do it."

"I'm sorry about that, but I really need to get this design finished so I can start adding the furniture. The paint looks like a flat white from Sherwin-Williams. And water dripped down on the wallpaper, too." She pointed to a spot under the molding, where the wallpaper took over after the paint. "That looks like Emma's Garden from Waverly's Cottage Series. It's a pretty popular wallpaper, so the hardware store should sell it, too."

I blinked. "Wow. You're the first person I've ever met who could tell me the exact name of my wallpaper."

She threw me the same patient smile I'd used with Stormie earlier. "It's my job. I work with wallpapers all the time. You'll need to get a roll of paper and a quart of paint. Kilz comes in a quart size, too."

"Gotcha. See you in a few minutes. And I think I'll lock the door when I leave so nobody walks in on you. I'm not expecting anyone until ten, but you never know."

I headed for the front of the studio, where I flipped the OPEN sign around and stepped outside. After locking the dead bolt, I walked to my car, parked in the third row. Although I hadn't planned to leave the studio so soon, sometimes these things couldn't be helped.

CHAPTER 11

I drove away from the parking lot on autopilot. By the time I arrived at Homestyle Hardware, my dashboard clock read 9 a.m., which was late by some people's standards, including every construction worker in Bleu Bayou.

Only a few pickups remained in the hardware store's parking lot: a cherry-red Chevy Silverado with a busted towing hitch.

It looked like Shep Truitt's car, which I'd spied at Dogwood Manor yesterday. Sure enough, Shep stood just behind the pickup, holding a beige plastic sack from Homestyle Hardware.

As I pulled into a parking space, I noticed he took a bungee cord out of the bag, then began to tie it over something in the truck bed.

"Good morning," I said as soon as I stepped out of my car and approached him.

He immediately whirled around. "Good...good morning." He tossed the bungee cord into the truck bed without securing it to anything.

"How are your fingers?" I asked.

"So-so." He lifted his injured hand in the air. "It kills me I can't use them for much. What're you doing here this morning?"

"I've got a little chore to do back at my studio. And you?"

"Nothing much. Well...it was good to see you again."

He turned slightly, but something about his tone sparked my curiosity.

"Are you still working at Dogwood Manor?" Although I assumed Mr. Solomon's death had put everyone out of work, I couldn't help but notice dusty fan prints marked the front of his Carhartt work shirt.

"Nah. The police roped off the place. Just like you said they would. I couldn't get back in."

"Then I guess you must have another job."

He scrunched his nose. "What makes you think that?" He followed my gaze down. "Oh...the shirt. I'm hauling some supplies this morning. Haven't landed another job yet, though."

"I'm sure you will soon." I took a step toward the truck bed, but he moved sideways to block my view.

"Well, looks like I should get going," he said.

At that moment, something light fluttered against my ankle. It was the discarded plastic bag, which ruffled around my feet. "You dropped something."

He bent to retrieve his sack, which gave me a moment to glimpse over his shoulder. Sure enough, he'd packed the truck bed with dusty architectural elements: everything from a stained-glass window with pink and green inserts to a pair of worn shutters. A wood corbel carved with the image of a dogwood blossom lolled next to the other items.

Sweet mother of pearl! I recognized the corbel immediately. It belonged to Dogwood Manor—one of several that held up the roof on the front façade. There was no mistaking the dogwood flower carved into its center. "Mr. Truitt?"

He forgot all about the bag and immediately straightened. "Well, I've gotta go. I have to haul this stuff away today. Lots going on. Guess I'll see ya later."

With that, he headed for the cab of his truck, then fired up the engine. The truck *whoosh*ed away in a cloud of dust and loose gravel.

How odd. I mulled over his strange behavior, not to mention the stash from Dogwood Manor in the truck bed, as I slowly picked up the plastic bag and walked through the parking lot. After tossing the rubbish in a trash can by the entrance, I stepped into the lobby of Homestyle Hardware.

I nearly bumped into a display of Scotts garden hoses on my way to the paint aisle. My mind kept replaying the strange scene. Why would Shep Truitt pack his truck with embellishments from the mansion? Especially since the police had sent everyone home yesterday afternoon and secured the area with crime-scene tape.

Lost in thought, I rounded the first corner I came to. It was an aisle dubbed "Paints and Primers," and I began to haphazardly scan the shelves for a can of Kilz.

"Hello, dear."

I turned to see Waunzy Boudin behind me. The grandmother held some strips of colored paper in her hand, which she waved in greeting.

"Hi, Mrs. Boudin."

Today she wore another flower-print sundress, only this one featured tiny sprays of violets that bloomed across the front. Like before, she wore bright pink flip-flops that matched her purse. She leaned close, and the oriental smell of Shalimar washed over me.

"It's so good to see you!" She hugged me tightly.

"Nice to see you, too."

"What brings you in today, dear? Are you finally going to paint that rent house you live in?"

"Huh?" Her comment brought me back to the present. Leave it to Waunzy to remember the color of the home I shared with Ambrose, or what the locals called a "rent house." Although I fancied the bubblegum-pink walls, which complemented a listing garden gate over the walk, she obviously didn't care for the color.

"I thought you liked pink," I said. "You know, because of your clothes."

"I do, dear. But not on a house. There are limits, you know."

"Actually...I'm not here for my rent house. I'm looking for something for my studio. Do you know if they stock a product called Kilz?"

"Of course, dear. Everyone loves that primer." She pointed to a spot on the bottom shelf, which I'd somehow overlooked. "There it is. You don't need much. If it's a small spot, I'd recommend you only get a quart."

I crouched close to the floor. "Thanks. It sounds like you're a real expert when it comes to this stuff."

"I've become quite the remodeling addict. You know, my dream is to renovate all the old mansions around here. Don't you think this color would look wonderful on Dogwood Manor?"

She stuck a strip of paper under my nose. Different paint colors stair-stepped down the paper, from warm toast to medium gray. She'd circled a color in the middle with a thick band of red ink.

"That color's pretty," I said as I straightened. "Is it taupe?"

"Yes, indeedy. It's called Tantalizing Taupe. I just love the name."

"You mentioned Dogwood Manor had been painted taupe before. It's so sad that Mr. Solomon passed away there yesterday, don't you think?"

She stiffened. Although I hadn't meant to change the subject, I couldn't talk about his property without mentioning his passing. "I mean, he won't even get to see the finished product. Now someone else will have to take over."

"If you ask me...well, never mind." She shook her head. "All I know is that Dogwood Manor was never meant to be painted pure white. That's not what the original plans called for. It's a shame no one ever pays attention to the history of these homes anymore. What's the point of renovating something if you're just going to whitewash it?"

"I suppose."

"I've got half a mind to repaint it myself." She stopped short, clearly flustered. "But don't pay any attention to me, dear. I'm just rambling now. Silly idea."

I glanced again at the strip of paint colors in her hand. She'd drawn so many circles around "Tantalizing Taupe" that ink zigzagged through a reference number at the top of the paper.

"I'm sure the heirs will sell the house once the dust settles," I said. "Maybe then someone else can fix it up the way it used to be."

"We'll see." Finally, she dropped her hand. "And here I am, going on and on. I've got a million things to do today, so I'd best skedaddle. Good to see you, dear."

She hurriedly threw me a smile before she backed away. In addition to the strip with different shades of taupe, she carried several brochures on coordinating trims and exterior stains. All of which seemed a tad excessive, since she'd admitted it was a "silly idea" for her even to think about how Dogwood Manor should be repainted.

Why would Waunzy drive all the way to the hardware store to pick out colors for a house she doesn't even own? Either she was bored, or she already had plans to restore the manor to its former glory. And Waunzy Boudin didn't strike me as the type who bored easily.

CHAPTER 12

Still lost in thought, I shopped a bit more, then wandered to the checkout line with my primer and a can of flat white paint in hand. Although the store didn't stock the Waverly wallpaper I needed, a manager offered to place a rush order for me. He promised the paper would be delivered to my studio later that afternoon.

Only one register was open by the time I finished shopping. Apparently, the hardware store closed most of its checkout lanes once the flow of building contractors dwindled to a trickle, and most of the cashiers now roamed the aisles, looking for shelves to restock or shopping baskets to retrieve.

Two other people waited in line ahead of me, so I took my place behind them and balanced my items on a nearby display shelf that carried Duracell batteries and aluminum flashlights. A voice interrupted my thoughts a few seconds later, since someone ahead of me had begun to argue with the teenaged cashier.

"What do you mean…you won't sell it to me?" the customer demanded.

"It wasn't supposed to be out on the shelves." The bespectacled high schooler wore a green apron festooned with the Homestyle Hardware logo, and she raised her voice, too, although her volume couldn't compete with the irate customer's.

She seemed to be caught between trying to placate the man and following the instructions of someone else, who stood behind her. The second gentleman had helped me order the Waverly wallpaper, so I knew he was one of the store's managers.

"But that's ridiculous!" the customer said. "Of course you have to sell them to me."

My gaze flew to the speaker. It was Cole Truitt, the familiar ponytail emerging from a hole in the back of his LSU ball cap. He sounded incredulous, as if he couldn't believe the cashier's insolence. He also waved a Visa over the credit-card machine, as if he was going to insert the card no matter what she said.

"But we're not supposed to sell them anymore. It was a mistake." The girl furtively glanced behind her, as if seeking her manager's approval. She got it when the manager gave her a terse nod.

"I'm really sorry," she said. "We should've pulled that kind of ant killer from the shelf a long time ago."

Cole blew out a puff of air. "*Pppfffttt*. This is ridiculous. The stuff was sitting right there in aisle five, next to the other bug killers. Give me a break."

Noticeably frustrated, Cole didn't budge his hand from the credit-card reader. It seemed the two speakers had come to a standstill, with neither side willing to compromise.

I lowered my gaze to the items in question. Cole had thrown two boxes of Grant's Kills Ants onto the checkout counter, a brand I didn't know. A large banner scrolled across the top of the boxes, clearly legible. BAIT TRAPS the type proclaimed, in all capital letters.

The purchase seemed innocent enough, but the hullaballoo elicited a loud sigh from the woman in front of me, who abruptly left the line by stalking away. She'd been waiting to buy a pack of Duracells and some gum, but she changed her mind when the argument apparently came to an impasse.

I, on the other hand, didn't have a choice. I needed the paint and primer for my store, so I dug in my heels, determined to pay for my items and hightail it out of there.

"Look, if you won't sell them to me, you're going to have to throw them away." Cole finally moved his hand from the credit-card machine, but only to balance his palm on the counter so he could lean forward.

At that point, the manager whispered something into the girl's ear, and her shoulders noticeably relaxed.

"Okay, okay," she said. "We'll sell them to you."

After a moment, Cole leaned away from the girl. "Well, that's much better." He brought the Visa back to the credit-card reader with a satisfied smirk and proceeded to swipe the magnetic strip against the machine. "It's what I've been saying all along. You should thank me for taking them off your hands."

The girl rolled her eyes, which Cole didn't notice, because he was so busy with the credit-card machine. The store's manager had slipped away by this time, as if happy to be free of the situation.

I felt sorry for the cashier, though, because she'd clearly been bullied into saying yes. I was about to tell her that when the girl addressed Cole again.

"That'll be four dollars and eighty-seven cents," she said. "Do you want a bag with it?"

"Nah. I'll just carry them out to my truck." Cole snatched the items up from the counter once the reader had finished verifying his information and he'd signed the keypad. He still hadn't noticed I stood right behind him, and that I'd heard every word.

"Thanks." The cashier thrust the receipt at him, as if he might grab that, too.

Once he left the store, I took his place and moved my items onto the counter. "What in the world was that all about?"

"He was crazy, wasn't he?" the cashier said. "We get people like that all the time. They think they own this place, and they'll never take no for an answer."

"You poor thing." I nudged the items closer, since I really did need to pay for them and hustle back to my shop. "Bless your heart."

"See, you understand. It's not my fault the store has certain policies. That guy made it seem like I just told him no for the fun of it."

"Certain policies?" I cocked my head. I'd checked out the boxes Cole wanted to buy, and they seemed innocent enough.

"Yeah." She lifted my paint can and swiped its underside with the scanner. "We got a notice about that product a while ago. No one's supposed to sell it around here, because it could be dangerous." She focused on the primer next, once more running the scanner along the underside. "Is that all you need?"

"Yes, that's all." I fished around in my clutch for my wallet. "What do you mean, dangerous? I thought those things were made of borax. Last time I checked, that was a detergent."

"I wouldn't know anything about that. All I know is my manager told me they used to make this kind with arsenic, so we're not allowed to sell it in the store anymore."

"Is that right?" My hand stalled inside the purse. *How very interesting.* Why in the world would Cole Truitt insist on buying a specific bait trap, when the store had so many others on the shelf that were less dangerous? It didn't make sense, unless he didn't know about the poison. And Cole struck me as the type who would know something like that.

"Yep. That guy took the last two boxes off the shelf," the girl said. "There's none in the warehouse, either. It seems like we never, ever carried it now, which is a good thing, really."

"You don't say." I resumed the hunt for my wallet, which was wedged up under the zipper. "Why did you guys ever carry it in the first place?"

"We didn't know. I remember when the manager told me we had to get rid of it. I threw away boxes and boxes. Someone probably stuck those two on a different shelf, and that's where he found them."

I pulled out my wallet and waited for her to give me the total.

"That'll be twenty-seven dollars and seventy cents," she said.

I handed the girl two twenty-dollar bills. "Hmmm. So, he cleaned out your entire supply?"

"Yes, ma'am." She quickly made change, after consulting an amount on the screen of her cash register. "At least we won't get in trouble now. Would you like a bag with that?"

"No, that's okay." I quickly picked up my purchases. "I'm just going to carry them right out to my car."

I threw the girl a smile as I headed for the exit. How odd of Cole to choose that specific product—one that was no longer available—and then clean out the store's supply. As if he knew someone might come looking for products that contained arsenic around here. Judging by his haste, he seemed to expect that to happen any day now.

I nearly ran into a sliding glass door as I replayed the scene in my mind. Luckily, I paused in the nick of time, then I nearly fell through the exit when the panels *whoosh*ed open.

The minute I stepped into the parking lot, the morning sun warmed my arms and neck, reminding me of the late hour. I'd need to skedaddle if I wanted to make it back to my store in time to work on the fixups before my client meeting at ten o'clock.

Shards of light glinted off the asphalt as I walked. I lowered my gaze to protect my eyes and blindly made my way to the car. Once there, I opened the door and tossed the cans onto the passenger seat before moving behind the steering wheel.

I didn't quite make it, though. At that moment, another car came rumbling down the aisle of the parking lot, almost nicking my car's frame with its enormous front bumper. I froze, prepared for the *ssscccrrreeeccchhh* of metal on metal.

But nothing sounded. The driver swerved around me at the last second, and the car slid sideways into an empty parking space across the way. The driver must've been distracted, because the parking lot was practically empty, leaving lots of space to maneuver around.

The sedan slowly \pulled away, its paint glinting like a fat drop of liquid silver. Not only did it look familiar, but it was missing a rearview mirror on the driver's side. *Oh my stars!* My gaze flew up—to the window. The same driver sat behind the steering wheel as before: a pretty, middle-aged woman with a trendy haircut and oversized sunglasses. The sunglasses never wavered as she stared straight ahead, which was amazing, considering she'd nearly smashed right into my trunk.

What were the odds I'd spy Herbert Solomon's pricey sedan not once, but twice, in the same week? That'd never happened before, even when the man was alive. Probably because he spent all his time at his construction projects, harassing his foremen or yelling at his work crews.

This time, though, I couldn't ignore the coincidence. I jumped into my car and fired up the engine, determined to find out who was driving Herbert Solomon's car. Even though I was in a hurry to get back to work, my curiosity got the better of me.

I threw Ringo into Reverse and quickly backed out of the parking space, grateful for the almost-empty lot. In a few seconds, I'd pulled in behind the Rolls, which caused the woman to glance from the windshield to her rearview mirror.

She revved the engine when she saw me, and the car pulled away. I did the same, until our bumpers nearly touched. We drove that way to the feeder road, neither of us willing to back down.

I kept pace with her for several miles. Fortunately no one else was on the road, since the morning rush hour had passed, and we sped to the outskirts of downtown. We approached the first stoplight, which signaled the start of the business district, and the light suddenly changed from yellow to red. I moved my foot from the accelerator and prepared to brake at the light.

She had other ideas. Instead of braking, she accelerated even more, and the Rolls zoomed through the red light, its back end fishtailing as it swerved through the intersection. After what seemed like an eternity, she finally made it safely to the other side, where she sped off again.

I merely gaped. I couldn't put my life—or someone else's—in danger, so I watched her disappear as I drummed my fingers against the steering wheel. By the time the color flipped to green again, the Rolls was gone.

Dagnabit. There was no telling where the driver had been, or where she was going. An unfamiliar brunette who was brazen enough to commandeer Mr. Solomon's Rolls-Royce only a day after his death. I'd have to tell Lance about our race when I returned to the studio.

I barely noticed the scenery on my drive back to the Factory. When I reached the parking lot at work, I found a space on the first go-round—hallelujah—then I hopped out of Ringo. I trundled my purchases, along with my purse and three stir sticks, over to Crowning Glory, where I dropped everything onto the welcome mat.

By now the building brimmed with life, as other studio owners, clients, and vendors walked back and forth from the storefronts to the parking lot.

I unlocked the front door and muscled the merchandise inside. It was time for me to spread the first layer of primer on the ceiling before my ten o'clock appointment and be done with it.

I wobbled over to the counter, fortunately without dropping anything. I almost knocked everything to the ground, though, when someone coughed nearby.

"Ivy?" I gaped at a woman who perched on the edge of my couch, wearing a pitch-black St. John suit.

"Hello, Missy. I didn't mean to scare you." She rose from the couch with a shy smile. "Some girl let me in after I knocked on the window."

"Whew. I thought I was seeing things. I'll bet you ran into my assistant or my interior decorator. My gosh, I haven't seen you in a dog's age."

Herbert Solomon's second wife had been one of the first people to greet me when I arrived in Bleu Bayou. We bonded one weekend at a "fancy hat" contest that took place at the hotel where her stepdaughter was supposed to be married. Although Ivy lived in Baton Rouge, she'd traveled back and forth between her home and the wedding venue at least twice a week for several months, and we became fast friends.

"I've been meaning to come and see you," I said. "I'm so sorry about your loss." While I longed to tell her about my strange encounter with her late husband's car, this didn't seem like the time, nor the place.

"Thank you." Her face fell at the mention of Herbert's passing. "It's funny, but I kept nagging Herbert to go to the doctor. I wanted him to find someone here, since he practically lived in Bleu Bayou while he was renovating Dogwood Manor. He didn't listen to me, of course. You know how difficult he could be."

Since my grandmother always said it wasn't nice to disparage the dead, I kept my mouth shut about that, too, but she didn't seem to notice.

"If I told him once, I told him a thousand times, 'You need to see a doctor. Go find out what's wrong.' He always told me he'd go the next day."

I hurried over to the couch and gave her a quick hug. "You poor thing. You must be in town to plan the funeral. Here, let's sit down again."

She nodded and sank onto the couch. "I'm organizing a small service for a few family and friends. But I wanted to visit my favorite hatmaker, too. I couldn't very well come all the way down to Bleu Bayou without saying hello to you."

"I'm so glad you did." I settled onto the cushion next to hers. Her face looked lined from this distance. Taut grooves surrounded her eyes and mouth, and a wisp of gray hair fluttered against her cheek. She still was beautiful, of course—nothing could change that—but her delicate features seemed more fragile now.

"It looks like I'm interrupting you, though." Her gaze wandered to the can of Kilz on the countertop. "I can see you're busy."

"Don't worry about that. The painting can wait a minute or two. I'm working with a decorator, and she sent me to the hardware store for some supplies."

"Is that the girl who let me in?" She brought her gaze forward again, but her stare was vacant. "A tiny thing in high heels?"

"That sounds like Erika Daniels. She's sprucing up the studio for a magazine interview tomorrow. Did you meet my assistant, too?"

"I think so. Pretty face, big earrings, brown bangs?"

"That's Beatrice. Looks like you met everyone."

"The first girl, the interior decorator, her name sounds familiar."

"Erika? Your husband hired her to decorate Dogwood Manor. She only got about halfway through the project before he died."

"I see." She shuddered, and the vacant look disappeared. "Can we talk about something else for a minute? I haven't heard any good news for days now. What's all this about a magazine interview?"

Since she seemed desperate for a diversion, I obliged. "An editor called me yesterday from one of the big bridal magazines in New York City. He wants to do a feature story about the shop, only it's not quite ready for its close-up, if you know what I mean."

"Then it's a good thing you have an interior designer. How's it working out?"

I shrugged. "Too early to tell. I just hired Erika yesterday. She's out of work now that the police cordoned off the mansion."

"I suppose. Wonder if I should call her and ask her to finish the project at some point? It'd be a shame to only finish half of the renovation."

Unfortunately, we'd already returned to the subject of Dogwood Manor, since we couldn't seem to avoid it. "She'd probably like that. Erika turned away other jobs so she could work on the mansion. And I know she needs the money."

Ivy's jaw subtly tensed. "Don't tell me Herbert refused to pay the poor girl."

Since Ivy would be the first person to admit that her late husband was tighter than the skin on a grape, I didn't feel the need to sugarcoat anything. "She didn't get paid...but it wasn't your husband's fault. His administrative assistant kept forgetting about it."

"His assistant?" Her face tensed even more. "I hope Herbert didn't make the designer work with Evangeline. That bimbo couldn't find her way out of a paper bag."

"I didn't catch a name," I said, truthfully. To be honest, Ivy's expression surprised me. I'd never known her to dislike anyone, much less one of her husband's employees.

She pursed her lips as if the name left a sour taste in her mouth. "I'm sure it's her."

"All I know is the assistant kept forgetting to pay Erika's bill. I hope I'm not speaking out of turn. You have so many other things to worry about right now. I never should've brought it up. I'm sorry."

"Nonsense," she snapped. "I'm glad you told me. I've been trying to get rid of Evangeline for weeks now. Herbert tried to defend her, but there was no defense for what she did."

"'What she did'?"

Ivy's face remained clenched. "I might as well tell you the truth. Evangeline threw herself at my husband. I got proof of it when Herbert left his cell phone lying around. The pictures that girl sent him! She never thought I'd see them, of course."

"You poor thing!" I tried to hide my surprise, but my tone, no doubt, gave me away. "Is there anything I can do to help you?"

"Not now. But if Evangeline comes to the funeral, I don't know what I'll do. You may need to bail me out of jail. You'd do that for me, wouldn't you?"

I started to chuckle, but stopped short when she didn't join me. "C'mon, Ivy. You don't mean that."

"Don't I? They were having an affair, Missy. There's no other way around it. I suspected something was wrong when he kept charging haircuts to our Visa bill. If you hadn't noticed, my husband was bald."

I couldn't help but wince. *Who in their right mind would have an affair with Herbert Solomon?* While I didn't mean to be cruel, it defied reason. "Are you sure about this, Ivy?"

"I know what you're thinking," she said. "But it's true. Apparently, she talked him into hiring her for his business because she wanted to get close to him. I know he doesn't look like much on the outside, but my husband was a brilliant man. And he could be charming when he wanted to be."

I rose from the couch, completely flummoxed by our conversation. "I'm sure she wouldn't dare show up at his funeral, so you don't have to worry about that. How about if I call you later?" While I wanted to help Ivy as much as I could, she'd given me a lot of information to process, and I needed some time to work through it. "Let's meet for lunch tomorrow. I know this great place in town called Miss Odilia's Southern Eatery."

She rose, as well. "I'd like that. You can reach me at Morningside Plantation. I'll be staying there all week."

Now, that makes perfect sense. Her late husband had bought that property, along with Dogwood Manor, for his portfolio of historic homes. And since I knew the general manager, she'd no doubt connect me to Ivy's room if I asked. "Sounds like a plan. I look forward to it."

"Me, too. It'll be like old times again." The wistfulness had returned, and Ivy stared vacantly into space. "Well, I should get going. I've got to stop by the funeral home and make some decisions. And a police detective keeps calling and leaving messages. Maybe I should visit him and see what he wants."

"Good idea." I reached for her hand. "Please swear you won't do anything rash in the meantime."

"Don't be silly. It was just wishful thinking." She tried to sound nonchalant, but her voice was high and tight. "I really wouldn't hurt that girl."

"Good, because she's not worth your time. Please remember that. We can talk more about it tomorrow."

I walked Ivy to the front door and watched her step out onto the sidewalk. Her black suit stood out against the pale concrete, like the feathers on a crow as it moved through a sugarcane field.

For some reason, though, Ivy didn't walk to the parking lot when she reached the end of the path. She turned left, instead, toward the building's lobby.

She quickly glanced over her shoulder, then she ducked through a plate-glass door. While she might've had other business at the Factory, the move seemed entirely spontaneous. *Please tell me she's not going to do anything rash.* Although the day was young, my heart couldn't take any more trauma.

CHAPTER 13

The workday passed in a blur after that. A parade of deliverymen tromped through the studio with furniture, accessories, and whatnot from places like Pottery Barn, Ethan Allen, and even a few antique stores in New Orleans. I rose my voice to be heard through the din, but it was hard to ignore the *bump*s and *bang*s and *thump*s that deliverymen made only a few yards away while I met with clients.

To make matters worse, an electrician almost toppled off his ladder at one point. He held an enormous crystal chandelier in his hands, but his foot slipped through the third rung and the chandelier swayed, so I dashed away from my appointment to help him. My nerves never quite recovered after that, and I muddled through the rest of the appointment before disappearing into the workroom, my sanctuary, for a little peace and quiet.

It was about time I focused on the projects at hand. One bride, in particular, had presented me with a unique challenge, which still baffled me. She planned to be married at dawn in an outdoor pavilion at Morningside Plantation, some six months down the road. Which meant the weather would be nice and cold by then, given February temperatures on the Great River Road hovered in the mid-forties.

To compensate for that, she'd chosen a heavy satin gown trimmed in faux fur at the cuffs and collar. She'd happily presented me with a picture she'd found in *Today's Bride*.

The girl wanted something formal, yet fitting for wintertime. Since a heavy satin didn't quite work with featherweight lace, though, I'd have to use another material to construct the veil.

I poured through my design books for at least an hour before I came up with a solution. Since the weather would be coldest at dawn, and her gown featured an off-the-shoulder design, it made sense to cover her head with something extra thick and warm. No need for her to shiver through her vows, especially since February normally also brought a heavy dose of morning mist.

The idea came to me bit by bit. I finally imagined a snowy faux-fur hat with a birdcage blusher to cover her face. I'd construct the blusher from Chantilly lace, a heavier weave, and scallop the edge for a bit of interest.

I sketched several renditions, my hand flying over the sketchpad. At one point, Bea poked her head through the door, but I waved her away.

Unfortunately, the minute I stopped to catch my breath, my eyes threatened to droop closed, so I'd rush to the Keurig machine and chug another cup of coffee. When I finally rose from the drafting table for the last time—exhausted, but exhilarated—I stood under the threshold of the door to the studio, which had fallen silent again.

Somehow I'd managed to control my curiosity about the shop during the day. It wasn't easy, what with the *bump*s and *bang*s and *thump*s, but I'd angled my drafting table away from the door and suppressed the urge to sneak a quick peek.

Erika had crept into the workroom once or twice to ask for my opinion, but it felt like a formality. I was a firm believer in letting creative people do their jobs without my interference, so I gently declined her offer and encouraged her to follow her instincts.

I fanned my fingers across my eyes now and carefully threaded my way through the studio. When I dropped my hand to flip on a light switch near the exit, the breath caught in my throat.

She'd outdone herself! The chandelier popped overhead like a starburst and bounced light from one mirrored surface to the other. Gone was my tired-looking studio, replaced by a glitzy, glamorous showroom, complete with mirrored walls, a silver-leaf pattern on the ceiling, and ice-blue velvet couches.

Everything was perfect, and no one would ever guess that deliverymen had rushed the furniture into the studio that afternoon. No doubt price tags still hung from the undersides of the couches and chairs, but I could remove them when I returned to work in the morning.

Satisfied, I left my shop through the French doors. Once I locked them, I made my way through the parking lot to my car.

The sun hung low on the horizon as I wearily pulled away from the Factory. Only a few other cars joined me on the highway, and even the flow of Marathon oil tankers that normally traveled this stretch of road had slowed to a trickle.

After a few miles, my eyelids began to droop closed again, even with myriad cups of coffee coursing through my veins, so I slapped my left cheek to shock my system awake.

Maybe it'll help if I focus on the scenery. Over there sat Miss Odilia's Southern Eatery, with its purple flower boxes full of zinnias and caladiums, not to mention a parking lot crammed to the gills with hungry diners. Odilia had opened the restaurant earlier last summer, after she'd successfully launched a sister property in New Orleans. Now Lance's mother was known by the locals for her chicken and biscuits, not to mention her love of passing along town gossip in the guise of "news."

Just beyond the restaurant lay Grady's donut store, which was home to the best beignets on the planet. Unfortunately, it'd be a *lllooonnnggg* time before I could frequent Dippin' Donuts again, since I'd suffered through a disastrous date with Grady that had squelched my desire for any more of his baked goods.

The bakery signaled the end of Bleu Bayou's business district, and it was followed by a row of modest ranch homes. Soon I'd come across the immense columns and the grand lawn of the Sweetwater mansion, but for now, the single-story brick houses were neither immense nor grand.

In fact, builders had focused on the working class when they designed the houses. Each featured a concrete driveway placed front and center, instead of soaring Doric columns, and crabgrass filled the lawns instead of the more elegant St. Augustine variety.

A Craftsman cottage followed the first three ranch homes, and it, too, had seen better days.

Although Waunzy Boudin spoke passionately about renovating the antebellum homes in Bleu Bayou, she apparently didn't feel the same passion for her own home. The brown Craftsman wore a tired roof with several bare patches, and a large crack split the concrete driveway in two.

Everyone said the property began to decay the minute Waunzy buried her husband. Since then, the house had seemed to fall apart little by little, until all that remained was the craggy roof with its missing shingles, the cracked driveway in need of patching, and a front door held together with duct tape and spackle.

I noticed the door just as the panel swung open and Waunzy stepped out onto the landing.

She'd donned a plaid apron since our last meeting, and it hung low on her hips as she struggled to pull something out of the house and onto the lawn. She'd also traded in her pink flip-flops for a pair of fuzzy slippers, and one of them fell off during the struggle.

I slowed the car for a better look, after first checking the rearview mirror. The struggle involved a metal sign of some sort, which was too heavy for her to manage. Waunzy tried to lift the thing over the doorjamb, but it wouldn't budge. I quickly pulled the VW curbside to offer my assistance. "Hey! Need any help with that?" I called, once I lowered the passenger window.

Waunzy's head jerked up at the sound. She looked confused, as if she didn't recognize my car. But the moment she saw me sitting behind the steering wheel, her expression changed.

"Oh, it's you. I couldn't tell who it was at first."

"Hope I didn't scare you. Need any help over there?" I jerked my head toward the open door and the heavy metal sign.

"Why, yes. That would be great." She sounded relieved. "Every time, that thing gets heavier and heavier. Do you mind helping me pull it onto the lawn?"

"Not at all." Once I put the car in Park and slid out from behind the steering wheel, I dropped the key in my pocket and made my way up the crabgrass.

"What is that thing?" I appraised the metal sign. It reminded me of something a Realtor might use for an open house.

Waunzy followed my gaze to the rusted metal. "Just something I picked up at Homestyle Hardware a while back. It'll let everyone know my rental unit is available again."

When she moved to grab one edge of the sign, I took hold of the other. "Okay...let's lift it on three," I suggested, since nothing else she'd tried had worked.

"Gotcha."

"One...two...three." Together, we lifted the sign a few inches and *whoosh*ed it over the doorjamb. Then we half-pulled, half-pushed the panel onto the lawn. After that, it was only a matter of hoisting it high enough to clear the crabgrass and moving it down the lawn bit by bit until Waunzy motioned for me to stop.

"It goes right here," she said, sweat appearing on her upper lip.

Even at this late hour, sunlight ricocheted off the sign and warmed the metal under my fingers. I quickly lowered the sign and wiggled my fingers to cool them.

"Does it work?" I asked, once we'd planted the sign in the grass.

"You mean the sign? I suppose. It's the only way I can let people know about the property without having to pay for advertising. Those folks at the *Bleu Bayou Impartial Reporter* want two hundred fifty dollars for a little-bitty ad on the back page." She scowled at the very thought. "Can you believe it? If I could afford that, I wouldn't need to rent out a room."

"Good point." I slapped my hands together to shake off the dust. At least the chore had woken me up. "Bet you get great exposure with the road being so close."

"Just hope it works. My last renter skipped town without paying his rent. Any of it. By the time I figured out what he was up to, he'd vanished without a trace. *Poof!*"

"That's terrible. Did you file a police report?"

"Why bother? He's probably halfway to Mississippi by now. That's how some people operate…they hop from one place to the next and never pay a dime."

"I'm sorry that happened to you. I'll try to spread the word about the unit being available. I'm sure someone would love to live here."

She smiled faintly. "Thank you kindly. My house isn't fancy, by any means, but it's clean enough and the AC's nice and cold." She paused, as if considering whether or not to voice her next thought. "You know, I count on those rent checks every month to help me pay my mortgage. 'Spose I'll have to go down to Louisiana First Trust and beg for mercy. One of these days, those folks are gonna throw me out on my ear."

"But don't you get a salary at the historical society?" The executive director of one of the town's only nonprofits should have made a hefty salary, in my opinion. But, then again, maybe it all depended on how much the city council was willing to pay.

"I wouldn't exactly call it a 'salary,'" she said. "More like a stipend. I kept threatening to get another job, but not too many people around here want to hire someone in her eighties."

She quickly corrected herself. "Her *early* eighties."

Interesting. How did Waunzy ever think she could buy Dogwood Manor if she couldn't even scrape together the mortgage on a Craftsman cottage? Was it just wishful thinking on her part, or something more than that?

"My daddy always said life isn't fair." She slapped the dust from her hands, as well. "Too bad it's more fair to some folks than to others."

I sighed, the exhaustion hitting me full-force. I'd run across enough problems over the past two days to keep me busy into the foreseeable future. There was no need to add another one to the pile, especially since there wasn't much I could do to help Waunzy.

"Like I told you, I'll mention your room to my friends," I said. "Maybe one of them is looking for a place to rent." I gave her my most encouraging smile before turning to leave.

"Just a second, dear."

Her hand shot out as she grabbed my forearm, her grasp surprisingly firm. "Have you heard anything about Herbert Solomon's murder lately? You'd think they'd have a suspect by now."

Surprised, I leaned away. "I…I know they're working on it. He was poisoned. That much they know. And they finally figured out which poison the killer used."

"They did?" Now it was her turn to look surprised. "What do you know… guess the old coot ticked off the wrong person this time."

"Guess so." I gently extracted my arm. "But I really have to get going. I haven't been home in ages, and I'm dead on my feet."

"Of course, dear. I understand." Contrary to her words, Waunzy's eyes still looked troubled. "Don't let me stop you. You young people need your rest. And thank you for helping me with the sign."

"No problem." I backed away, careful to tuck my arms behind my back. "Good luck with finding a renter."

I finally turned when I reached the edge of the asphalt, and then I ducked through the driver's-side door of my car. Waunzy appeared in the rearview mirror as I pulled away from the property, wearing the same dazed expression I'd noticed when I'd first arrived.

The next few minutes passed in a blur as I thought about our conversation. Clearly, Waunzy was in dire straits, which didn't jibe with her plan to buy Dogwood Manor. Maybe she was just delusional when it came to the property, or maybe she intended to solicit investors in her bid to buy the mansion. Either way, I was much too tired to worry about it now, especially since I spied my own cottage once I drove past the Sweetwater mansion.

The thought of seeing Ambrose again propelled me out of the car as soon as I'd pulled into the driveway and parked. That, and something more unusual, which I noticed as I made my way up the walk. The faint smell of cooked sausage simmering on a griddle reached me halfway through the trek.

The smell grew stronger as I stepped into the cottage, making my mouth water since I'd forgotten to eat or drink anything since that morning except those cups of coffee and some nondairy creamers.

I picked up the pace when I spied Ambrose in the kitchen. He'd donned his favorite camouflage apron, which featured the words GRILL SERGEANT across the front. I snuck up behind him and planted a big kiss on the back of his neck. "You're a sight for sore eyes."

He immediately turned and smiled. "Hooray…you're home. I tried to call you, but no one answered at your studio."

"We probably couldn't hear you. We had people coming and going all afternoon, and, trust me, they didn't tiptoe."

Once I finally stopped talking, he leaned forward to give me a proper kiss. His lips tasted like spicy rice and Cajun sausage.

"Please tell me you made jambalaya," I said. "If you do, I'll give you anything you want."

"Anything? Anything at all?" He smiled crookedly. "Now, there's an interesting thought. But let me pour you a glass of wine first." He nodded toward an open bottle on the counter. It was a Duckhorn Vineyards merlot, one of my favorites. "We can drink it while I mull over your offer."

"Sounds good to me," I said.

He reached for a wineglass and began to pour from the bottle. "Tell me when."

I waited for the wine to reach the tippy-top of the rim. "Okay...now. Thank you."

"You obviously had a rough day."

"Yeah, but the studio looks amazing." I carefully sipped the wine, which tasted like blackberries and just a hint of aged oak. "I think we're ready for tomorrow."

He pointed to the kitchen table. "That's great. Go ahead and have a seat. The meal's almost done."

I gladly did as he asked and moved to the table, which he'd set with woven rattan placemats, porcelain soup bowls, and a burnished-silver ladle from the Bleu Bayou flea market. "You outdid yourself," I said. "And I'll bet you had a hard day, too."

"For only part of it. One of my clients tore her hemline when she was getting her picture taken. I fixed it for her, but she forgot to bring in the right shoes, so we have to meet again in the morning so I can check the length."

He poured the jambalaya into a white soup tureen with curlicued handles, which he brought to the table. He then ladled a generous serving of the dish into my bowl, while I waited.

"I hope you like it," he said. "Odilia La Porte gave me the recipe yesterday. I called her to say thanks for packing us those lunches. I don't know about you, but she gave me her jambalaya, and it was out of this world."

I peered into my bowl, which held browned sausage, chopped parsley, and sliced carrots. Yesterday's lunch was a faint memory, but I seemed to recall a plastic container filled with something very similar, which I ate before the fried chicken and biscuits. "I forgot about that. It *was* delicious. But how'd you find the time to shop for ingredients?"

The carrots and parsley looked fresh, but with the frenzy of the wedding season, our refrigerator hadn't held a fresh vegetable for months. He shrugged. "Odilia sent one of her waiters over here with some groceries. What? Don't give me that look. She *wanted* to do it."

"Okay, but I think she has a crush on you." Far be it from me to look a gift horse in the mouth, though, so I took a sip of wine while I waited for the food to cool.

"That's okay with me. Just as long as she likes one of us, we're gonna eat like kings."

"True. And it smells delicious. I kinda forgot to eat lunch today." He shot me a look. "I was worried you'd do that. I almost brought you some, but I got tied up with that client. Don't tell me...you didn't take a nap, either."

"Guilty." Maybe if I continued to sip from my wineglass, I could figure out a way to turn the conversation away from me and my forgetfulness. It was worth a shot, so I took another long, slow drink.

"You can't keep going like this, Missy." Apparently, Bo couldn't be swayed so easily. "One of these days, you're gonna crash. And then what'll happen?"

"I know, I know." I took another hearty swig, then held out my glass for a refill. At this rate, I'd fall asleep at the dinner table, but the alcohol was beginning to blunt the sharp edges of my thoughts and paint the room a soft, rosy color.

Besides, I had enough guilt to keep me going for a while. It'd started when I had to explain to Erika Daniels why I couldn't spare even a few minutes to patch an obvious water stain on the ceiling of my studio. The guilt only intensified when I spoke with Ivy, whom I should've visited months ago but never did. "Hey, I had a surprise visitor today."

"Really? Who was it?" Bo refilled my glass and passed it back to me.

"Ivy Solomon. She was married to Herbert, remember? I made a veil for her stepdaughter a few years ago, and you made the wedding gown." I set the wineglass next to the jambalaya, which finally looked cool enough to eat. After scooping up a mouthful of parsley, carrots, and andouille sausage, I savored the taste before swallowing. "This is wonderful. Anyway, she came by the shop to say hello."

"Too bad you guys had to reconnect because of someone's death. I remember she was really nice to work with on the other project."

"Yeah, I really like her. She came to town to plan her husband's funeral. But I've gotta tell you, she kind of worried me."

"Worried you? Why?"

"Because of something she said." While I didn't want to gossip—okay, maybe a little—I wanted to share my newfound information with Ambrose. It'd be all over town tomorrow anyway, since that was the way "news" worked in Bleu Bayou...it flew at the speed of boredom.

I leaned forward. "She told me her husband was having an affair with his hairdresser. Apparently, he hired the girl to be his administrative assistant without asking Ivy."

"You're kidding." Ambrose chuckled. "That old dog."

He obviously didn't understand the gravity of the situation. "I'm serious, Bo. Ivy was fit to be tied. She basically said she'd hunt the girl down if she ever ran into her in a dark alley."

"People say stuff like that all the time when they catch someone having an affair. She probably just wanted to vent."

"Maybe." I lifted the spoon and tried another bite of jambalaya. Little by little, the dull ache in my stomach had eased, until I almost felt normal again. Better than normal, actually.

"I don't think you have to worry about his widow. She'll have so much stuff to do between now and the funeral, she won't have time to think about his mistress."

"I hope you're right." Maybe some more wine would convince me, so I took another sip from my glass.

"But let's not talk about her. This is the first romantic meal we've had in weeks. A quick lunch at Miss Odilia's doesn't count." Ambrose lifted his wineglass to meet mine for a toast, which I sloppily reciprocated. "Here's to us."

"Whoa." Some of the wine sloshed from my glass onto the table. "I think I messed up your place mat. Sorry 'bout that."

"No problem. But I think you're already kinda tipsy, sweetie. Hope you didn't forget about your offer."

"My offer?" I crinkled my nose, the details of our conversation growing fuzzier by the moment. "What offer was that?"

"You offered to do something nice for me, since I made you dinner. Don't you remember?"

"I did?" To be honest, I couldn't remember much of anything at that point. What with the heaviness of my head, which felt like a ten-pound sandbag, and the warmth of his body next to mine, it was all I could do to stay upright. Finally, I gave in to temptation and laid my cheek on his shoulder. "Sure, I remember now," I lied.

"Uh-oh. Are you falling asleep on me?" Ambrose brushed my cheek with his thumb. "I had really big plans for us. And they involved that little pink number with the lace thong."

"You love that one, don't you?" I smiled sleepily and nuzzled his shoulder with my nose. "Let me rest here for a minute. Just one minute. And then we can play."

While I wanted to keep my eyes open, my body apparently had other plans. I nuzzled his shoulder again, grateful for the silence and the feel of his shirt beneath my cheek.

"*Heelllooo?*" he whispered. "I'm definitely losing you."

His voice sounded far away now, as if he'd moved to the other side of the room. Which was impossible, because his cotton dress shirt still tickled my skin.

"One minute," I mumbled. "That's all." Much as I hated to drift away, my thoughts pulled me further and further from the kitchen. After a moment, even the sound of Bo's breathing grew faint.

I gradually surrendered to the darkness. After all, what could possibly happen while I closed my eyes for just a moment or two?

CHAPTER 14

My eyes gradually opened again, nudged awake by pale sunlight that broached a nearby window. The room had brightened to a rosy glow by the time I lifted my head to take in my surroundings.

Apparently, I'd spent the night on our farmhouse bench in the kitchen. Above me was a wooden ledge, which looked suspiciously like the underside of the kitchen table. Around my shoulders lay something soft and warm, the fabric imbued with the smell of sautéed onions, cayenne pepper, and cooked meat. Since the smell was a bit much for the early hour, I pushed the material aside—it turned out to be Ambrose's favorite apron—and slowly straightened.

While I expected to see pots, pans, and dirty dishes crammed into our sink across the way, only a pair of yellow Rubbermaid gloves hung over the faucet like wilted dandelions.

Bless his heart. Not only did Ambrose cook me the best meal I'd had in ages—although I probably drank twice as much as I ate—he'd even cleaned up the mess afterward.

And how did I repay him? Not by enjoying a romantic evening with him, which we both desperately needed, but by literally falling asleep at the table. I winced, and it had nothing to do with the kink in my neck. Bo deserved better than that, and I made a mental note to break out his favorite negligee the very next chance I got.

Stiffly, I rose from the bench. Tangerine sun poured through the window over the sink, which meant the morning was still young. As I shuffled through the door to the hall, I glanced at the clock over our key holder. *Six o'clock. Perfect.* I had time to shower, change clothes, and eat a light breakfast before I headed out to the Factory.

Sweet mother of pearl! The Factory. Today was Wednesday. And not just any Wednesday, but the day a magazine crew would descend on Crowning Glory. Somehow, between the wine and Ambrose's thoughtfulness, not to mention his throaty whispers afterward, I'd managed to forget all about the photo shoot.

The details came rushing back. I was supposed to meet a crew at the shop in exactly three hours. A crew with professional-grade camera lenses, microcassette recorders, and enough New York City angst to work us all into a frenzy.

I yelped and headed for the bathroom, suddenly pressed for time. I remembered to call out to Ambrose at the last minute. "Morning, sunshine!"

Nothing answered but a songbird in the backyard, which meant that my boyfriend was already gone for the day. He'd probably tiptoed through the house as he gathered his things for work, which was one more reason for me to break out that negligee when we both got home tonight.

I ducked into the bathroom, quickly showered, and then changed into my favorite white Boss suit, which I paired with a turquoise camisole. To add more color, I roped a citrine necklace around my throat and added some matching orange slides. The white suit would complement my hats and veils without competing for attention, while the orange accessories would provide a pop of color against the pale background.

Once dressed, I grabbed a breakfast bar and a water bottle from our pantry, then I zoomed out of the house, started up the car, and pulled out onto the road. By now, the sky was a crisp aquamarine, but only a few eager beavers joined me for the trek to work. Rush hour didn't officially start until seven, although the term hardly applied to Bleu Bayou's sprinkling of minivans, oil tankers, and Fed Ex trucks.

Ten minutes later, I arrived at the Factory. Three vehicles already sat in the parking lot: Ambrose's black Audi, a white minivan that belonged to the building's resident florist, and a delivery truck with its back door wide open.

I entered the lot and whizzed into a space several aisles behind the truck. No need to take a front-row spot, which I liked to save for paying customers and the vendors who kept me supplied with netting, seed pearls, and whatnot.

I quickly checked my makeup in the rearview mirror once I'd parked, then I added another coat of lipstick for good measure. Even though the photographer wasn't due to arrive for several more hours, I was ready and primed for the day ahead.

The air was steamy when I stepped out of the car, so I didn't dillydally as I made my way to the studio. The welcome mat was freshly swept, since I'd seen to that little chore when I closed up the studio the night before. With a grin, I turned the handle on the French door and stepped into the studio. My joy lasted exactly one second, until the orange slides pressed against the floorboards with a sickening *squish.*

Uh-oh. Floorboards are not supposed to squish.

Horrified, I glanced down, where undulating planks surrounded my feet. The ground was a crazy Hot Wheels track that careened up and down, from one side of the studio to the other.

Somehow, sometime during the night, water must've accumulated beneath the planks and loosened the glue that held them to the concrete foundation.

I almost buckled, too, once I figured that out. At the last second, I reached for the door handle and gripped it for dear life, until the feeling passed. Then I tossed my purse and keys onto a display table at the front of the store, plucked off the slides, and began to tiptoe gingerly across the floorboards. Each step brought another *squish.* Not only that, but water had soaked the hems of my brand-new couches and stained the edges two shades darker. Repelled by the sight, I tried to stare at the ceiling as I hopscotched across the room and slid into the workroom.

Along with the *squish* of my toes on the floorboards, I now heard a new sound, a *whoosh* of water that came from the workroom's sink. The door beneath the basin hung open, and a stream traveled down the pipe and through a crack in the elbow joint.

Sure enough, I must've left the water running all night. Probably after I refilled the coffeemaker for the umpteenth time, since I'd made enough cups of it to satisfy a small army.

Deflated now, I made my way to the sink and slapped the faucet off. The water stopped flowing and the *splish-splash* disappeared, although it was much too late to do any good.

I wanted to scream, but how could I? It was *me* who'd forgotten to turn off the faucet. *I* was the one who hadn't noticed the crack in the pipe until it was too late. And it'd now be up to *me* to call the magazine crew at their hotel and tell them to stay put. Tell them they'd wasted their time when they hopped on an airplane and traveled all the way down to Bleu Bayou. They really hadn't needed to stay in a Quality Inn last night, where the best thing to eat would be a soggy waffle or a bruised banana this morning. Everything was ruined, all because of my negligence.

After cursing softly under my breath, I whipped out my cell to check the time. The minutes seemed to be speeding by, and already the screen read 6:50 a.m. D-day was a little over two hours away.

Maybe I should run next door and fetch Ambrose. Then again, odds were good he wouldn't know what to do, either. He didn't know anything about plumbing or carpentry. The same could be said of Beatrice. She could arrange hat displays and work with customers all day long, but she sure didn't know her way around a jackhammer, a crowbar, or an elbow joint.

My next thought seemed a bit more practical. I knew a perfectly good contractor who happened to be out of a job right now. A man with the tools, and the know-how, to fix this mess. And if he couldn't do it, he might know someone else who could.

Shep Truitt, the foreman at Dogwood Manor. Even though he'd surprised me yesterday by stashing a corbel from Dogwood Manor in his truck bed, I didn't have any other choice at this point. My suspicions about him would have to wait until after the crisis passed.

There's only one problem. I didn't know how to reach him. We'd never exchanged phone numbers when we met up at the hardware store, or at the mansion on Monday.

Just when I was about to give up, inspiration struck. I quickly dialed the number for the police station, and Lance picked up after the second ring.

"Good morning. You're up bright and early."

"Hey there. No time for small talk. This is an emergency."

A heavy sigh sounded over the phone. "Please don't tell me you found another dead body. I just got started on the Solomon case."

Although it was worrisome that Lance equated my phone calls with dead bodies, that was neither here nor there at this point.

"Don't worry. It's something else. Did you get the phone numbers for all of the workers at Dogwood Manor on Monday?"

"Of course I did. I'm interviewing each of them. Why?"

"Then you must have a number for Shep Truitt. He was the construction foreman there." I took a deep breath to buy some time. The trick would be to give Lance enough information to convince him to give me Shep's number, without letting him know why I needed it.

"You sound awfully evasive, Missy. What's up?"

"Okay. Here's the deal. I walked into my studio this morning, and everything's a mess. The whole floor buckled in waves of flooding water."

He whistled under his breath. "How in the world did that happen?"

"I kinda left the faucet running in my workroom last night. Don't say it. I didn't mean to leave it on…it was an accident."

"Missy, Missy, Missy."

I could only imagine the way he shook his head. "I told you not to say it," I snapped.

"Hey...you're the one who called me."

Then again, fighting with Lance wasn't going to help my case. "I'm sorry. I'm just mad at myself because I screwed up. But there's more to the story. A magazine crew will be here in a couple of hours, with a photographer. May I please have Shep Truitt's phone number?"

"I dunno..."

Since he sounded on the cusp of a "yes," it was time to push a little harder.

"I really need your help, Lance. The magazine story's a big deal for me. A huge deal. It's the best thing that's happened to Crowning Glory all year long."

"Okay, okay. I get it. This is important to you. And you've helped me out more than once, so I guess I owe you."

"Thank you."

After a moment of silence, Lance rattled off a phone number, which I quickly memorized. I repeated it back to him for good measure before telling him good-bye.

Once we both clicked off the line, I tapped the phone number I'd memorized onto my screen and waited through a few rings.

Finally, a sleepy voice sounded on the other end. "Ye'lo."

"Mr. Truitt? Good morning. It's Melissa DuBois. We met yesterday, remember?"

"I'm sorry. Who's this?"

"Melissa. All my friends call me Missy. I met you a few days ago at Dogwood Manor, and then we saw each other again in the parking lot at the hardware store."

"Yeah. That's right." He yawned loudly, a *whoosh* of air over the line. "What can I do for you this morning, Miss DuBois?"

"It's a long story, but did I catch you at a good time?"

"I guess so. I've got nothing going on right now. Matter of fact, I was sleeping."

"Then I'm sorry I woke you, but there's been an emergency at my hat studio. I got to work this morning, and the hardwood floor is ruined. One of the pipes leaked all night long."

"That'll do it. Those floorboards don't like water."

"Unfortunately, I found that out," I said. "Look, I need someone to come in and fix it. Quickly."

"How quickly?" He sounded wary, but curious.

"Ridiculously fast. I have a photographer coming here at nine." I waited for the inevitable groan.

"You mean nine tonight, right?"

"No…I'm talking about two hours from now."

The silence was deafening. After several beats, he finally spoke again. "You got me at a good time, actually. I don't have anything else going on this morning. Or the rest of the week, as a matter of fact."

"I'm so glad!" My voice squeaked, but I didn't care. "Not about you being out of work, I mean. That's not good. That's bad." *Focus, Missy. Focus.* I closed my eyes so I could concentrate. "But I'm glad you can help me out this morning."

"Not so fast."

My eyes popped open again. *Uh-oh.*

"I won't be able to glue the boards back down in time," he said. "That would take at least a few hours to dry."

"Really?" Apparently my squeal had been premature. "Then, how can you fix it?"

"Your best bet is for me to pull the floor up. Get all the wet wood out of there. It'll leave you with concrete, but that'd be better than warped floorboards."

My mind worked overtime as I thought about it. The "industrial chic" look was undeniably hot right now, and lots of designers purposefully left a building's foundation exposed as part of the design. Maybe the option wasn't so bad, after all.

"If that's what you think is best," I finally said.

"I do. I've got a crowbar and some industrial fans I could bring over. Should be able to pull those babies up pretty fast. Especially if I bring some help."

"Help?" While one part of my brain—the practical part—wanted to ask how much the extra "help" would cost me, the other part didn't care. "Okay. Do what you think is best. I'll try to stay out of your way while you work. How fast can you get here?"

"Is ten minutes fast enough?"

"Definitely. Bring whatever supplies and people you need. I'm so grateful for your help, but right now we're running out of time."

CHAPTER 15

I clicked off the phone line just as something else sounded in the studio. I shoved the phone back in my pocket, then I tiptoed across the floor to the door of the workroom. After peeking my head through the doorway, I spied Beatrice in the shop's foyer, her mouth agape. Next to her was Erika Daniels, who wore the same, incredulous expression.

"What happened?" they cried in unison.

I moved into the studio, the boards squeaking beneath my feet. "We sprung a leak last night back in the workroom. But I've got Shep Truitt coming over. I'm gonna flip on the air conditioner for him."

"You mean the foreman at Dogwood Manor?" Erika had yet to look up from the floor. "He's coming here?"

"Thankfully, yes. He said he can rip up the floorboards before the magazine crew gets here. I'm sorry, Erika, but water ruined some of the furniture, too."

Her gaze immediately flew to the velvet couches. "I see what you mean. But I don't think they're completely ruined. I can tack up the hems, and no one will see the stains today. They might even look better without that extra panel at the bottom."

Thank heaven for small miracles. "That would be great."

"What can I do?" Finally Beatrice was ready to join our conversation.

"There's a product I've been dying to try," Erika told her. "It's a stain from that company called Quikrete. We can roll it onto the concrete to give it a marbled look. You can help me with that."

"Gotcha," she said.

My gaze took in the studio. The blue velvet couches, the mirrored walls, the shiny surfaces in between. "Do you think that would look good with your design?"

Erika nodded. "I do. And the first coat only takes an hour to dry. You're supposed to do a couple of coats and a sealer, but we don't have time for that. Can you go to the hardware store and get some?"

"I suppose so." Thank goodness, once again, for Homestyle Hardware and its early-morning hours. "I'll go right now."

"Okay. We need a gallon of Quikrete stain in light gray." She paused a moment, as if thinking through the steps. "Two paint rollers, with poles, for use to swirl on the stain. We'll also need a paint pan and a few pairs of gloves. That oughta do it."

"Got it. Do you want to come with me, Beatrice?" I asked.

"I'd better stay here and help Erika with anything else she needs," she said. "Where do you want me to move the furniture?"

I quickly gathered my purse and keys. "Well, Ambrose is already here. Go next door and see if he can help you carry the furniture into his studio while Mr. Truitt rips up the floor. That's our best bet right now."

"Got it. Good luck at the store," she said.

I said good-bye, then moved to the exit. I glanced at my white clutch at the last minute, which reminded me of something else.

"Think I'll grab some coveralls while I'm at it," I said over my shoulder. "Staining a floor in a white pantsuit sounds like a bad idea."

I hurried outside and jumped into Ringo. Then I floored the accelerator all the way to Homestyle Hardware. After finding the supplies, I whipped out my credit card and paid for the purchases.

The sun was brighter than ever when I emerged into the parking lot, tossed my bags in the backseat of Ringo, and then hightailed it back to work.

The parking lot at the Factory looked much different now. A line of cars queued up to enter the gate, and drivers inside cruised up and down the aisles, their necks craned expectantly.

Once I entered the lot, I circled it twice before I found a space in the last row. Then I parked and muscled the packages past line after line of cars, including a bright red Chevy Silverado that sat in the second row.

Hallelujah...the cavalry's arrived. Even with my prayer answered, I still approached the door to Crowning Glory cautiously, since I had no idea what I'd find inside.

The welcome mat, which had been so carefully swept, was gone, replaced by an industrial fan set to high. The machine churned air into the studio, the noise a dull roar, like an airplane engine idling. Over that sound came the sharp *crack* of splintering wood, which was enough to make me want to drop the packages and run.

Which I didn't do, of course. Instead, I gingerly stepped around the fan and entered the studio.

I barely recognized the place. Everything below the waist was gone. The new coffee table, the velvet couches, the glossy hat boxes arranged as a side table. Nothing remained but a pile of splintered wood, a set of open toolboxes, and sheets of wavering plastic that ruffled over the walls and ceiling. Even Beatrice and Erika had disappeared.

"Hello?" My voice got lost in the noise.

Two men crouched over the floor in front of me, but neither of them turned.

"Excuse me!"

That did the trick. Shep glanced up, then flipped off the circular saw in his hand. Meanwhile, the other man set his crowbar on the ground without turning.

"Hey there." Shep leaned back on his haunches, his face streaked with sweat and sawdust. "You're right...the floors were a mess."

"What did you say?" I yelled.

Since I still couldn't hear him, I quickly turned around and flipped off a switch on the back of the fan. Not that I wanted to interrupt their work, but the bags from Homestyle Hardware had grown heavier and heavier while I waited for someone to notice me.

"The floors were a mess," he repeated, once the fan shut off. "We're almost done pulling them up. It wasn't hard, since the water loosened everything."

Hooray for more miracles. "Where do you want me to put these bags?"

He looked at me quizzically, so I hoisted my purchases higher.

"Is that the stain for the floors?"

"It is. I got everything Erika said she'd need. Where do you want me to put it?"

"Bring it around back." He jerked his thumb over his shoulder. "Cole here will help you with that."

Cole. Of course. The other man was Shep Truitt's son, the one who had handed me a water bottle in the hall at Dogwood Manor, not to mention the one at the scene at the hardware store yesterday.

"By the way," Shep continued, "I think you'd better let *us* stain the floor."

I lowered my arms again. "Are you sure? I thought the designer wanted to do a pattern in the stain by herself."

"We already talked about it. She wants it marbled. We—me and Cole here—have done that a thousand times before."

Relief washed over me. "That'd be great! I'm sure we could do a million other things in the meantime."

"Hey, Cole," Shep called over his shoulder. "Help the lady with her bags."

"Yes, sir." Cole rose and picked his way across some rubble. "Can I give you a hand with those?"

"Thanks." The minute I gave him a few bags, I noticed angry red slashes on my wrist from the plastic handles.

The foreman's son didn't seem to mind the weight, though, because he grabbed the bags and casually hopped over the fan. I fumbled after him, once I turned the fan back on, and then I emerged into the bright sunshine of the parking lot.

"Thank you." I hurried to catch up with him. "I don't know what I would've done without you and your dad to help me."

Cole casually swung the packages. "It's no problem, really. I'm kinda glad you called, to tell you the truth."

"Glad? Don't tell me you think this is fun."

"I know it sounds crazy." He grinned. "But we love this kind of stuff. There's nothing like doing demo first thing in the morning."

"Whatever you say."

We soon approached the corner of the building that shielded the employee parking lot from view.

"I was really afraid your dad was going to say no," I continued.

"He doesn't have much choice. Ever since my dad's construction business went bust, he's had to take any job he could find. Even the ones he doesn't want."

"You mean like working at Dogwood Manor for Mr. Solomon?"

"Of course. That's the only reason my dad would put up with his crap." He swung one of the bags extra hard, and metal clunked against asphalt. "A year ago, he would've told the old man to take a hike. But he's got too many bills now."

"That's too bad."

"It's not just that. There's more to the story."

We rounded the building and stepped into the lot where employees kept their cars. At least a few of them, anyway. Most people didn't trust their vehicles to the pebbly, cracked asphalt.

"What happened?" I asked.

"My dad put up with way too much guff from the old geezer, and then the guy stiffed him. Can you believe it? That Solomon had some nerve."

"He stiffed him?" I nodded to the back door of my studio. "But I thought he had an assistant who paid all the workers."

"That was his excuse, all right." Cole's easygoing gait had grown stiffer with each step. By the time we reached the back door, his brisk stride matched mine. "Truth is, the guy never intended to pay my dad. Everything came to a head at the end."

"Let me guess…somehow your dad figured out Mr. Solomon wasn't going to pay him." I dropped the plastic bags and turned, my curiosity piqued. "What tipped him off?"

"A few things." He dropped his packages, too, and the metal can once more *thunk*ed the asphalt. "But the kicker was when my dad found Mr. Solomon's cell phone in the bathroom at the mansion."

"Really?" Although he was a whiz with business, Mr. Solomon didn't take very good care of his phone. If he had, Ivy never would've found out about the affair between him and his hairdresser. And now this.

"Yeah…my dad saw a text from the old man's assistant. Apparently he told her to find someone else to finish the job at Dogwood. He was going to fire my dad, only he didn't have the balls to do it face-to-face. And for what? Dad wasn't responsible for the project delays or the cost overruns. Solomon kept changing the specs on him. The nerve of that guy!"

Cole yanked open the back door, which sent it banging against the wall. He stormed in ahead of me, apparently forgetting all about the bags on the ground.

"You forgot your supplies," I called out.

He returned a second later and glanced at me sheepishly. "Sorry. I get worked up when I think about it. Bullies like that make me wanna puke."

I paused, mid-stride. His words sparked another memory—one of the encounter at Homestyle Hardware yesterday. Hadn't I thought the very same thing when I heard Cole argue with the cashier? He'd seemed all too ready to take advantage of the girl's age and inexperience in order to get his way.

"Just a second," I said.

He threw me a backward glance. "Yeah?"

"I happened to be in Homestyle Hardware when you got into an argument with the cashier yesterday. What was that all about?"

The sheepish look returned. "You saw that, huh? Not one of my finest moments, I'm afraid."

"You really lit in to her. What was the big deal with the ant traps?"

"Here's the thing." He leaned close, as if prepared to share a secret with me. "Not a whole lot of people know this, but that ant killer is the only thing on the market that really works. It's magic. It'll kill ants you didn't even know you had."

"But the girl said the stuff was dangerous. Aren't you worried about using arsenic at your house?"

He shrugged. "It wasn't for my house, it was for my garage. And I don't even have a pet. Plus, I don't like being told what I can and can't use on my personal property. It doesn't sit right with me."

He suddenly turned and began to walk away, our conversation over.

Something about the explanation didn't ring true, though. I'd have to ask him about it later when I wasn't so pressed for time.

I reluctantly followed him into the workroom, where I stacked my sacks next to his on the sink. Cole had moved to the studio, and his voice rang out as he hollered for his father. At that moment, something else sounded. It was my cell phone, which I'd stashed in my pocket. I withdrew it and glanced at the caller ID before tapping the screen.

"Hey, Lance."

"Hi again." Lance's voice was warm, despite my earlier snappiness. "I'm over here at Dogwood Manor, and I found something interesting. Any chance you're up for a little drive?"

I glanced down at the raw concrete, which looked like a sheet of old, scraped dimes. "Actually, you're calling at a good time. The contractor's here with his son, and they're going to marble the floor of my studio. So, I have to stay off of it for at least an hour."

"Good. Then head on over here, and I'll meet you on the second floor."

"Uh-oh." I remembered something else. "Not so fast. I might have to help Erika and Beatrice move furniture. They're working on it all next door, at Ambrose's place."

"Okay, then. But if you find out they've got everything under control, I sure could use your help. I found something, but I don't know what to make of it."

Hard to say what made me feel better: having Lance ask for my help, or hearing the *whoosh* of a ShopVac when Shep and Cole began to suction debris off the floor. Either way, I probably could spare a few minutes away from the mess, and it might even turn my morning around.

CHAPTER 16

After checking in with Erika and Beatrice next door, who swore they didn't need my help to fix the watermarked couches or to organize accessories, I headed for the parking lot to find my car.

I'd just missed Ambrose, who was on his way to Baton Rouge to visit a certain wholesale fabric supplier. Apparently one of his clients had purchased designer shoes with six-inch heels, even though her dress only included a two-inch hem. It'd take him most of the morning to track down extra fabric and fix the girl's mistake.

Since I had no reason to linger at my shop, I quickly drove to Dogwood Manor, where I spied Lance's Oldsmobile as soon as I arrived. The car wore its usual layer of dust and grime, along with a film on the windshield where the cleaning fluid couldn't quite wash away the muck.

I parked next to the jalopy, then hopped out of my car. The scaffold on the east side of the manor's façade looked skeletal now, with no construction workers or extension cords or heavy-duty power tools to fill it.

Around me, an eerie silence took the place of the *clank*s and *whir*s and *bang*s. The only other sound came from a few cicadas, who took advantage of the shade offered by the rosebush near the front door. Two days had changed everything.

I headed for the stairs once I entered the house. When I reached the top, I paused on the second-floor landing to take in the view. Even unfinished, the mansion had beautiful bones, with smooth plaster walls that provided a blank canvas for artwork, a turreted ceiling that looked like something from a Grimm Brothers' fairy tale, and a wide hallway that led to the mahogany-paneled library. Such a shame no one could work on the renovation now, since it was so close to being finished.

No doubt Ivy, Herbert Solomon's widow, would take possession of the mansion at some point. Then again, Shep Truitt could place a lien against the property until he received his fee. Erika Daniels could do the same thing. The possibilities were endless, and none of them boded well for the beautiful mansion.

Once I took in the view, I moved to the east hall, where I spied an open door at the very end, above the library. I approached the door and saw Lance standing there, a pile of moving boxes and wooden pallets all around him. He stood with his back to me, as he read from something in his hand.

"Hello." I spoke softly, although we were the only two people around.

He whirled around. "Great. You're here. Come on in." He motioned for me to enter by waving his hand.

The room was cavernous. A domed ceiling rose high above our heads, its surface painted with a giant mural of a riverbank scene. The picture was awash in blues and mauves, and it depicted an old-fashioned paddle wheeler with gingerbread fretwork that separated the upper and lower decks. The handrails all wore the same patriotic bunting, which was striped red, white, and blue.

"The ceiling's beautiful," I murmured, surprised to find something so finished in the otherwise bare room. "What room is this?"

"Looks like this was supposed to be a master bedroom. And that's nothing." Lance indicated the packing boxes all around us with another sweep of his hand. "I've been sitting here, going through this stuff. It looks like Solomon ordered a brand-new bedroom suite months ago."

"Is that what you wanted to talk to me about?"

"No. This is."

He stepped toward me and handed me a piece of paper, which bore the unique typeface for Harrods of London. It was a receipt for purchases made in January—a full eight months ago. Under a line titled "Remit," someone had written the princely sum of 690,000, which was almost $800,000, followed by Erika Daniels signature.

"*Holy schmolly.*" I gave a long, low whistle. "Erika spent almost a million bucks on bedroom furniture! How is that even possible?"

"Apparently, you have to shop at Harrods. But that's not what I want to know." Lance looked confused as he glanced around the room. "Why didn't Solomon just stay up here? It looks like he started to, since some of the boxes are open, but he never moved in."

I followed his gaze. Sure enough, someone had pulled a mattress off of a pallet, but they'd left the plastic wrapping on. "I see what you're saying.

Why did he use that dinky room downstairs, when he had all this wonderful stuff waiting up here for him?"

"Not only that, but why did he spend so much for this room in the first place? Everyone told me he hated to spend money. He doesn't seem like the type of guy who'd splurge on furniture that no one else was going to see."

"I may be able to answer that one." I slowly walked over to the mattress, which was angled to the wall, and ran my hand along the plastic. After dusting it off, I sank onto the nearest corner. "I'll bet he was planning to use this room with his mistress."

Lance puckered his brow. "What do you mean, 'his mistress'?"

"That's right...you don't know, do you? Ivy Solomon came to visit me yesterday. She said she caught her husband having an affair."

"And you didn't think to tell me that?" His squint hardened to a scowl.

"I'm sorry, but I forgot. I was dead on my feet yesterday, since I'd worked all night on Monday. It won't happen again."

Gradually, the scowl softened. "Okay, then. You need to let me know stuff like that. So, what's all this about a mistress?"

"His wife said he'd hired his hairdresser to be his administrative assistant. But she found out later the girl was his mistress."

"Do you have a name?"

I shook my head. "Ivy wouldn't tell me. But she did say she was going to call you. She's gotten all of your messages."

"Good. I'll add that to my list of questions for her."

"It's the only reason I can think of for the expensive bedroom furniture." I glanced again at the beautiful ceiling overhead. "Someone once told me Herbert Solomon forbid Ivy from ordering new curtains for their house in Baton Rouge and she had to sneak behind his back to buy them. Sheesh."

"Maybe your guess is right, then."

"It's only a theory, but it makes sense." I rose from the mattress. "Well, I should get back to work. Unless you need me for anything else..."

"No. I think we're good. I'm gonna lock up the room and then I'll walk you out."

I moved to the door as Lance pulled a plastic bag from his back pocket. After dropping the receipt into it, he folded the bag into thirds and shoved it back in place.

Neither of us spoke as we walked along the hall toward the stairs. As soon as we reached the landing, Lance's cell phone broke the silence.

Once he pulled the ringing phone from his pocket, he squinted at the screen before answering it. "Detective LaPorte here."

Some mumbling on the other end, which I couldn't decipher.

"I see," he finally told the caller. "How'd you get my name?" He shifted his weight forward as he listened for a moment. "Thanks for letting me know," he said. "I'll check it out as soon as I get back to my office. I really appreciate the call."

He nodded at something else the caller said, then punched a button to hang up the phone. "Well, that was interesting."

I tried not to look too curious, since I didn't want him to think I'd been eavesdropping on his conversation. "Really?"

"Yeah. That was some lady from New Orleans. An antiques dealer."

My ears pricked up. "You don't say." One of my hobbies was searching for antiques in the narrow shops that lined Royal Street, since the city was chock-full of antique treasures. "Why would an antiques dealer from New Orleans call you?"

"She said she saw something last night on eBid that bothered her." Lance slipped the phone back into his pocket. "Somebody put a bunch of architectural items on sale there."

"That's nothing new. The site has a whole category for architectural salvage. People put tons of stuff on it."

"Yeah, but the lady said she found a corbel that belonged to Dogwood Manor."

"Don't tell me…it was carved with a dogwood flower."

Now it was his turn to look surprised. "Yeah. How'd you know that?"

"I saw a corbel just like that in Shep Truitt's truck yesterday. We ran into each other at Homestyle Hardware. It was sitting right in his truck bed, and he tried to hide it from me."

A moment later, I grimaced. I'd forgotten to tell Lance about *that* encounter, too. No doubt he'd berate me for forgetting to tell him something else.

"*Miiisssyyy.* You've got to start letting me know about those things. Everything you hear about Dogwood Manor…everything you see…it's all part of the investigation."

I did my best to look contrite. "I really am sorry, Lance. I mean it. Everything's been out of whack since Mr. Solomon died. I know it's no excuse, but it's the only one I've got."

Slowly, he exhaled. "Okay. How did you know the corbel came from Dogwood Manor?"

"Because it had a dogwood blossom carved on the front. It must be the same one the lady told you about on the phone. And Shep acted really paranoid when I tried to check it out."

"According to the antiques dealer, the emblem was pretty recognizable. She knew Herbert Solomon had died, and she wondered why someone would strip parts from the mansion only a day later."

"So she called the police?"

"She wanted to warn me about all the scavengers who steal things down here, which I already know about. People will take anything and everything that's not nailed down from those old mansions. They even take statues and stuff from the cemeteries around here. She thought someone probably stole the corbel from Dogwood Manor and then placed it up on eBid to make a quick buck."

"That'd explain a lot. So, what're you going to do?"

"First things first. I need to bring Shep Truitt into the station for a little conversation. Then I'll have to get those things pulled off eBid. They're all part of the Solomon estate."

I glanced at my watch. More than thirty minutes had elapsed since I'd left the Factory. Hopefully, Shep and Cole had finished staining the floor by now. While I cared about Lance's police investigation, I also cared about a certain photographer who was due to arrive at my studio soon.

"I need to get back to my shop," I said. "And that's where you'll find Shep."

"I think I'll follow you over there."

"That'll work."

With that, we both bounded out of the mansion and headed for our cars. It was a good thing Lance had affixed a light bar to the roof of his car, because he needed the extra help to keep up with me.

CHAPTER 17

Thankfully, we both arrived at Crowning Glory in one piece, and I threw open the door to the studio to find a beautifully stained floor. I quickly glanced around and spied Shep across the way.

"Mr. Truitt?" I called from the doorway. "Someone's here to see you."

Shep glanced up. "It's okay. You can walk on the floor. The stain dried a lot faster than we thought it would."

Nevertheless, I plucked off my flats, then tiptoed over to the counter, where I lightly hopped up on a bar stool that'd been put back in place.

The floor looked wonderful. Swirls of gray approximated the wavering veins that ran through a slab of marble, and the color deepened from light to dark, with most of the stain hitting smack-dab in the middle.

Lance also tiptoed to the counter, which made me smile, given his height. He reminded me of a giraffe trying to pussyfoot from one marbled rock to another without falling through a crack.

"Could you come here, Mr. Truitt?" Lance said, once he reached the bar stool next to mine. "I'd like to speak with you for a moment."

When Shep noticed Lance, he immediately frowned, but he did as the detective asked. "Is something wrong?" he said, once he reached the counter.

"I got a call this morning." Apparently, Lance wasn't going to waste any time on niceties. "A very disturbing phone call. Someone placed things on eBid last night that looked like they came from Dogwood Manor."

Shep's gaze flew to me. "And you think I took them? Is this because of what you saw yesterday at the hardware store, Missy?"

"It is," I said.

He'd already figured out the reason for Lance's questions. Not only that, but he didn't deny being involved in the transaction.

"I told Detective LaPorte we saw each other at Homestyle Hardware and that you had some pretty interesting things in the back of your truck."

"I got those things from the Dumpster." Shep sounded insulted.

"So, the corbel *did* come from Dogwood Manor?" Lance asked.

"Of course it came from there. But it'd been thrown away."

Lance looked askance. "Why would anyone throw it away? Those things cost a lot of money."

"Because it was the corbel that fell on my hand." Shep raised his right hand and lightly wiggled his fingers.

Only then did I notice the missing bandage. Although bruised, Shep's fingers moved freely, as if they'd never been smashed.

"My hand is gonna recover, but the corbel got damaged. The bottom broke completely off of it when it fell down in my truck."

"What was it doing in your truck in the first place?" I asked.

"I was going to repair the underside. The wood was rotted clear through the bottom. But someone hauled it to the Dumpster while I was at the ER, so I never got a chance."

"But there were other things in your truck," I said. I'd spied a whole stash of architectural elements back there.

"All headed for the Dumpster." Shep pulled a key ring from the pocket of his jeans with his other hand. "We can go out to my truck right now. Some of the stuff is still back there. You'll see...it's too damaged to use. People will buy the stuff anyway, though, because they all want something antique-y to put in their gardens."

Lance quickly rose. "Let's go, then. I'd love to see what else you have back there."

I didn't budge. While I wanted to help Lance with the investigation, the clock was speeding toward the top of the hour. If I didn't watch out, a photographer would show up on my doorstep before I had a chance to put the studio back together again.

"I can't go, Lance. I've got to fix this place up before the magazine crew gets here."

At that moment, the front door banged open and I gasped, certain my fears were about to be realized.

"Good morning." Erika Daniels strode into the room with a large bag in her hand, and Beatrice loped in behind her.

"Thank goodness." I clasped my hand to my chest. "It's only you."

"Nice to see you, too." Erika smiled, but she stopped when she noticed Lance. "Uh-oh. Has something happened, Officer?"

"Just asking some questions," Lance said. "I'm working on Herbert Solomon's murder case."

"What a horrible thing to happen," she said. "And to think it happened right here in Bleu Bayou. I hope you catch the person who did it."

"He's working on it." I studied the bag in her arms. "What'd you bring us?"

"It's something from my own house." She pulled a faux-fur blanket out of the sack, which she unfurled. "It'll look great on one of your new couches, and I can bill you for it later."

"It's pretty. Hey, Lance. Before you go...could you help us move a few couches over from next door? It'll only take a second, since I know you're in a hurry."

Lance shot me a look, but he hustled next door to help move the furniture anyway. The minute the couches hit the floor, he vanished, anxious to join Shep and investigate the contents of the man's truck.

By the time Beatrice and I wrangled the couches into the perfect position, and Erika finished adding her accessories, the studio looked wonderful.

"Everything looks beautiful." I plopped onto a couch, relieved beyond words.

"It does look good, doesn't it?" Erika nudged a table lamp to the left. "I'm going to take a few pictures for my portfolio before the magazine people get here. And don't let me forget to give you the bill before I leave."

At the mention of money, my chest tightened. I never did ask Erika for an estimate, and now it was too late. *But really...how bad can it be?* Plus, there'd be plenty of time to deal with the price tag once the magazine crew was gone. I could study the invoice then and maybe slide a few things around in the budget to make it work.

"Thank you, Erika. You really saved my hide."

"Don't mention it." Something dark flittered across her face. "I wish Mr. Solomon was here to see all this. He never thought I had good taste."

"That can't be true. If it was, he wouldn't have hired you to decorate Dogwood Manor."

"Yeah, but he watched my every move. I had to get his approval for everything. Everything! Plates, tablecloths...you name it. It was like being twelve again and having to ask my dad for an allowance."

The memory of a pink receipt from Harrods fluttered through my mind. It wasn't exactly the type of purchase someone made who was worried about her employer's approval.

She continued, oblivious to my stare. "Maybe the magazine story will make it all worthwhile, though. They might even ask me to do freelance work. Wouldn't that be something? I'd better hurry if I want to get those pictures."

While Erika took her photos, I moved back to the counter to check the schedule. The minute I finished, the door to the studio once more burst open.

"Hello, hello, hello." A burly man in a jaunty porkpie hat slipped over the threshold.

"Greetings!" I plastered a giant smile on my face as I stepped out from behind the counter. "We've been waiting for you. Love the hat!"

The man, obviously a photographer, given the professional-looking Nikon strung around his neck, made his way to the sitting area, where he dropped a tripod next to one of the couches. He was followed by a pale, thin woman who wore trendy eyeglasses and a thick black braid.

"You must be Melissa DuBois." The woman bypassed her associate and approached the counter. "I'm Daphne Lewinsky. I'll be interviewing you today."

When I moved to greet her, I noticed the smell of cigarette smoke. "Nice to meet you, Daphne. Everyone loves your magazine." Which was true, so I didn't have to embellish anything. "Where would you like to do the interview?"

"Do you have a table we can use? I need to set my notepad on something hard."

"Sure, follow me." I was about to lead her into the workroom when I remembered something else important. "Where are my manners? Miss Lewinsky, I'd like to introduce you to Beatrice Rushing. She's my assistant. I couldn't run this business without her."

I motioned to Bea, who grinned at the recognition. While the two women shook hands, I pointed to the very back of the room, where Erika stood with her cell phone, snapping pictures. "And over there is Erika Daniels. She's the interior decorator who created this beautiful space."

"Well, it's lovely. Nice to meet you." Daphne shook Erika's hand. "We won't keep you guys any longer than necessary. I've got a list of questions I need to run through, and then I'd like to speak with one of your clients. You know, to include a quote from an outside source, so it's not just the two of you talking about the studio."

"Of course," I said. "Beatrice, could you please rustle up Stormie Lanai's telephone number and give it to Miss Lewinsky?"

Beatrice nodded, while I explained the choice. "Stormie's a local newscaster. We just finished working on a fascinator for her wedding."

Daphne jotted the name into a Moleskin notebook she carried. "Good. I'll need to talk to her today, if possible."

"That should be fine. Stormie's getting married in Las Vegas, but it's not until this weekend, so she should be around. She might be able to give you an interesting perspective, since we had to remake her hat from scratch." The writer glanced up. "Any chance I could get a glass of water, too? I really don't know how you guys put up with this weather."

I squelched a smile, since I'd heard that comment my whole life. First in Texas, where I was born and spent my childhood; and then in Nashville, where I went to college; and now in Bleu Bayou. "You get used to the heat and humidity after a while. Beatrice, could you bring Miss Lewinsky some water, too?"

"You got it," she said.

In the meantime, I escorted Daphne to the workroom. The place looked completely different now. The old cherrywood drafting table was gone, replaced by a sleek, modern one in glass and chrome. Kind of like the Mies van der Rohe couches in our building's lobby, made with straight lines and hard angles.

A few ergonomic office chairs sat by the table, and I offered one to Daphne. I sank into the other one as she got settled.

"Tell me a little bit about your company." She shifted, and the chair squeaked. "Whatever made you set up shop down here?"

I squelched another smile, since I'd been asked *that* question a thousand times before, too.

"Bleu Bayou kind of found me, to be honest," I said. "I thought I was going to stay in New York City once I graduated from Vanderbilt. You know, the whole story about small-town girl making good in the Big Apple? But a funny thing happened after graduation."

I leaned back in my chair as the memory washed over me. Even though it'd taken place seven years before, I could still smell the diesel fuel on the tarmac at Louis Armstrong New Orleans International Airport.

I'd flown in from my miniscule apartment in New York City, where I worked as an intern for a famous fashion designer who had more hutzpah than talent. The man loved to send me on pointless errands, just so he could feel important, and to change my schedule on a whim.

In March of that year, he ordered me to visit New Orleans Fashion Week. He'd recently become enamored with jazz, and he'd planned to launch a line of women's ready-to-wear with flapper dresses and wide-legged pants.

So off I went. It was the first time I'd visited Louisiana, and it turned out to be a turning point in my career, although I never suspected it at the time.

The memory continued to unfurl, as if it'd happened only yesterday. Halfway through the week, after running from one fashion show to the next, I'd decided to take a break. I'd ditched out of the last show early, with my right hand aching from the nonstop sketching and note-taking. Somehow, I ended up on Canal Street. I remember ignoring the trash that lay in the gutters and the smell of urine in the alleys, because I was so enamored with the quaint storefronts that lined that historic street. So quaint, I spent hours going from one shop to the next, until I finally arrived at Feathers and Lace, one of the oldest hat stores in the country.

The window display had stopped me in my tracks. It was pure perfection: framed by a pink-and-brown awning and a display of women's fascinators that floated on heavenly clouds. Since I'd created Derby hats for many college friends, I'd become semi-knowledgeable about the art of hat-making. But that visit to Feathers and Lace marked the first time I realized someone could actually build a successful business around hats, veils, and accessories.

The next few hours had sped by, I recalled. The owner, a sweet octogenarian who'd moved to New Orleans in the fifties, had convinced me to visit the Great River Road, which she thought offered limitless possibilities for anyone brave enough to open a hat shop there.

Apparently, brides had recently rediscovered the old mansions that lined the Mississippi River, and they were eager to spend their wedding budgets on elaborate ensembles to match the opulence of the homes.

I took the shopkeeper's advice and visited Bleu Bayou the very next day.

"And that's how it all started," I told the reporter. I noticed she had stopped taking notes by now, and her pen lay idle. "I'm sorry. Am I speaking too fast?"

"No, not at all." She leaned close. "I think it's so interesting to hear about people who actually follow their dreams. You know, I wanted to be a novelist at one point."

"That's wonderful! Why didn't you?" The writer struck me as the type of person who could accomplish anything once she set her mind to it.

"I was too chicken," she said. "The magazine gives me a steady paycheck and insurance benefits. I always thought I'd write my novel at night, when I wasn't working. But somehow that never happened."

I nodded, since I'd become acquainted with several folks who'd thought they could pursue a passion at the end of the workday, only to find they barely had enough energy to make dinner, let alone create something.

"It's never too late," I said. "You could still do it."

"I suppose." She furtively glanced at a watch on her wrist. "And I'd love to talk to you more about it. But I really need to get back to my questions.

So, after you launched your studio, was there ever a point when you thought you weren't going to make it?"

"Of course." I shrugged, since it all seemed so simple in retrospect. "I wondered what would happen if I fell flat on my face. But then I met the shopkeepers who worked here, and they became a kind of support group for me."

No need to mention I'd also taken up with one of those shopkeepers, who happened to own a studio right next to mine. Ambrose was another reason I'd felt so at home in Bleu Bayou, but I wanted to keep my private life to myself for now.

"Let me tell you about hat-making." *Time to change the subject.* "That's why you're really here, isn't it?"

"I suppose. It seems to be a lost art. Do you think hats will ever make a comeback?"

"Well, I can't speak for men's hats, since haberdashery is a whole 'nother field. But I'm pretty sure women's hats are coming back in fashion, especially for special occasions like garden parties and weddings."

Together, she and I flipped through my sketch pad, while I began to explain the process for turning a fanciful idea into an actual hat or fascinator. I even included a little history lesson about women's headwear.

"Do you know why we call a hatmaker a milliner?" I asked. "It's because shopkeepers in Milan, Italy, would supply the ribbons, laces, and bows back in the old days."

"I never knew that." She jotted another note in her book, and then we chatted a bit more about hat-making.

Finally, after forty minutes or so, she softly closed the notebook's cover. "Well, I think I have everything I need for the story."

"Great. Could I offer you one of my hats before you leave? It'll protect your face from the hot sun out there."

She pondered the offer for a moment. "Well…I don't normally take gifts from my sources, but it might inspire me while I'm copywriting. Sure. Go ahead and show me what you had in mind."

We left the workroom and walked into the studio. By now, the photographer was done with his pictures, and he gave us a nod as we approached.

"I've just got one more picture to take. I need a head shot of Melissa."

My hand flew to my hair, which wasn't surprising, given the morning I'd had. "Do you mind if I run to the ladies' room first? I haven't checked a mirror all morning."

"No problem," he said. "I've got to set up a backlight anyway. We might want to use a couch over there. It'll be good for what we need."

He indicated the sitting area by the front door. Nearby was a table full of straw picture hats, which I pointed out to the writer.

"Any one of the picture hats on that table would look wonderful with your long hair. Please feel free to try some on while I run to the restroom."

"Okay." She tentatively reached for a sisal hat with a satin headband as I walked by her.

Once I ducked into the restroom, I fingered my auburn hair and mentally perused my stock of hats, since it wouldn't do for a milliner to appear in a photo bareheaded. Then I dusted off my jacket and pants, which were still white, praise the Lord, and reentered the studio. Daphne stood by the display table with a confused look on her face and nothing in her hands.

"Here, let me." I scooped up the perfect sisal hat for her once I reached the table. "We call this style a 'picture hat' because it circles your face like a round picture frame."

I placed the hat on her head, and then I gently retrieved a hat pin from the gold satin headband, which I used to secure the hat to her braid. "At one time, women were told they should wear this style with full skirts, to balance everything out, but now people wear picture hats with pretty much anything."

I smoothed a bump created by the hat pin, and then I gently turned her toward a three-way mirror.

A broad smile broke out on her face. "It's beautiful. And it's not too wide, so I could wear it in the city."

"That's why I picked it out. Normally, I'd suggest a fascinator for you, since New York City has such tight spaces. But that wouldn't help you with the sun."

While she appraised her reflection, I automatically moved to a different display, which held various fascinators and hair combs. I picked out one with silk Chinese rose petals and ostrich feathers, which I balanced on my head before smoothing the comb in place. By now, I knew each of my designs backward and forward, and I could easily affix a hat to my head without checking a mirror.

I met the photographer in the sitting area afterward, where he took about a thousand pictures of me from every angle. That was how it felt, anyway, since my cheeks smarted by the time he finally capped the lens.

"Got it," he said. "You have a great profile. Have you ever thought about modeling?"

"Not really." I held my breath while he lifted his camera bag off the ground. Thankfully, none of the gray stain had rubbed onto his bag, which was my worst fear.

"Well, you should," he said. "Even if you're not six feet tall, you can still work as a catalog model."

"Thanks, but I think I'll stick to hats. I love what I do."

"Suit yourself. It was nice working with you."

Once the photographer left with Daphne, who now had Stormie Lanai's telephone number *and* a brand-new hat, I sank onto the bar stool by the cash register and carefully unthreaded the fascinator from my hair.

"Hallelujah and pass the mustard," I said. "I thought they'd never leave. That was fun, but it was exhausting."

"I don't know how you do it." Beatrice slid onto the bar stool next to mine. "I'd crack up if someone took that many pictures of me."

"You get used to it after a while. It's weird, but I almost forgot he was there. He told me to lift my chin once or twice, but that was it. By the way...thanks for helping me out."

"No problem." She snapped her fingers when she remembered something. "I almost forgot...Erika had to leave. She dropped an invoice for you over there." Beatrice pointed to the cash register, which had a piece of paper propped against its keys.

I warily stood. "Now comes the reality check. I have no idea how much she charged me for all this stuff."

Head ducked, I slunk toward the invoice and pulled it off the register. I purposely held it at arms' length as I returned to the bar stool.

"I can't do it. You look at it." I thrust the paper at Beatrice, as if it might burst into flames. "Break it to me gently."

Once she took the paper, Beatrice gasped, which said more than any words could.

"That bad?" I tried to peer over her hand, but she'd pulled it away.

"'Fraid so. Guess we need to reopen Saturday afternoons again." She slapped the bill onto the counter, facedown.

That's impossible. I'd spent two long years working overtime so I could afford to close the studio by noon on Saturdays. I treasured that time off, since it was my only chance to run errands in town, like everyone else.

"You're just being dramatic. I'm sure it's not that bad." I flipped the bill over, then let out a gasp as loud as Beatrice's. "There must be some mistake."

A line of zeros jumped off the page. The final bill came to $55,000, including $45,000 for furniture and $10,000 for accessories.

"How...how could that be? How could this furniture cost so much?" My gaze ping-ponged around the room, until it landed on one of the velvet couches. "She must've done the math wrong. There's no way everything added up to that. No way!"

"Okay, calm down. Maybe you could get her on the phone, and she'll explain everything."

Something moved at the door just then, and I turned to see Ambrose wander in.

"Explain what?" he asked innocently.

"You're back!" I rushed to meet him, my troubles momentarily forgotten. "I'm so glad you came home." I gave him a big hug to show I meant every word.

"I was only gone a few hours."

"I know, but it felt like forever."

We remained locked in our embrace until Beatrice delicately cleared her throat.

"Sorry." He pulled away. "So, Missy. Tell me all about the interview this morning. How did it go?"

"Good." I quickly corrected myself. "I mean, great. I wouldn't change a thing. The reporter took tons of notes, and the photographer got loads of pictures."

"So, why don't you look happy? You should be thrilled to have that behind you." He indicated the floor with a nod. "Plus, it looks like you got new floors in here. I had no idea you wanted to refinish them."

"I didn't want to," I said. "The studio flooded last night and Shep Truitt made an emergency house call." My chest tightened again at the thought of Shep Truitt and all the equipment he'd brought. "I guess that's another bill I'll have to pay..."

"C'mere." Ambrose gently took my arm and guided me back to the bar stool at the counter. "Now, sit down and tell me everything. What happened?"

I did as instructed and weakly sank onto the chair. Somehow the furnishings around me began to lose their luster, given the hefty price tag. "The designer is charging me forty-five thousand for the furniture in here. Can you believe it? I don't have that kind of cash, Ambrose. And there's no way I can come up with it in thirty days."

"Don't forget about the accessories," Beatrice added, unnecessarily. "That's another ten grand."

I shot her a look. "Thanks for reminding me, Bea. But it's beside the point. It doesn't matter if it's fifty-five thousand or fifty-five million... I still don't have that kind of cash on hand."

While I wanted to bolt from the studio right then, and run as far and as fast as my legs would carry me, Ambrose didn't flinch.

"The way I see it, you have two choices," he said. "You can go back to the designer and question the bill. Or you can send all this stuff back."

"Send it back?" I hadn't even thought to return the merchandise.

"The furniture was the biggest chunk of the bill," he said.

My gaze once more swept the room, but this time I mentally cataloged the items. Truth be told, they didn't amount to much. A pair of couches, a coffee table, a few crystal lamps. All of it magnified by shiny mirrors that lined the walls. There was nothing I couldn't replicate by going online and snooping through some Internet shops. Of course, I'd still have to make Erika a custom Derby hat for her fee, like I'd promised, but I could try to return the furnishings, once I did my best to restore it all to its original condition.

"By the way"—Ambrose turned to face Beatrice—"do you mind if I steal your boss for an hour or so? I want to get her out of here and maybe buy her some lunch."

"Okay by me." Beatrice shrugged. "Bring me back something to eat, and it's more than okay."

"Deal. Let's get out of here, Missy. It sounds like you've had a long morning."

"Just a second." A memory niggled at the corner of my mind. "I think I promised Ivy Solomon I'd meet her for lunch today. Let me check my phone. Maybe she left a message."

I moved behind the counter to retrieve my clutch. Sure enough, the screen on my cell showed a missed call from Ivy, along with a text message. Apparently she'd been delayed at the funeral home and needed to reschedule our lunch date. Just when I was about to slip the phone back into my clutch, the ringtone sounded. Not only that, but the screen showed the caller's identity.

"Uh-oh," I said in a stage whisper. "It's Erika Daniels."

Cautiously, I tapped the phone's screen. "Hello, Erika. What's up?"

"Hi, Missy. Did you have a chance to look at my bill yet?" She sounded far too perky for someone who'd just handed me a bombshell.

"About that—"

"The terms are net thirty, so you have a whole month to pay it off."

"I'm afraid there's a problem," I said. "I have to send all this stuff back. It's beautiful, but I can't afford it."

"Excuse me?"

I took a deep breath. "I love what you did with the studio. I really do. But I'm afraid I don't have that kind of cash right now."

"Then why did you hire me?" Her sharp tone caught me off guard.

"I...I honestly didn't know everything was going to cost so much. I thought you were going to use stuff I already had." While I didn't want to argue with her in public, I also didn't want to be a pushover.

"You should've told me that up front." She practically spat the words. "Now I'm stuck with a bunch of expensive furniture I don't need."

"Can't you return it?"

"Maybe, but this will kill my reputation with my suppliers. No one's going to want to work with me after this. I can't believe you did this to me!"

"Look, I said I was sorry." Unlike her, my voice remained level. "I don't know what to tell you. Believe me, I'd love to keep the studio exactly as you designed it. Maybe someday—"

At that, Erika abruptly hung up, and it took me a moment to realize she'd ended the call.

"My gosh," Beatrice said. "What happened? You look shell-shocked."

Slowly, I lowered the phone. "She told me off...that's what happened. And then she hung up on me."

"That's very unprofessional," Ambrose said. "She should've given you a chance to explain."

"She didn't want to hear my explanation. She froze me out the minute I said I couldn't afford her furniture."

"Okay, then." Ambrose offered me his arm. "Let's get out of here. I want to get you away from all this craziness for a while. It won't kill you to take a break, and it just might save your sanity."

I walked through the studio in a daze. While the call from Erika Daniels was over, I had a sinking feeling that my troubles with her were not.

CHAPTER 18

By the time I reached Ambrose's car, the cloud hanging over my head had begun to lighten. Leave it to him to make me feel better, even though I'd still have to deal with Erika when I got back to the studio.

"Thanks for getting me out of there, Bo." I waited for him to open the car door, and then I ducked inside. "You always know how to cheer me up."

He smiled as he rounded the hood of his Audi and whisked open the driver's-side door. "No problem. It'll be good for you to take a break."

We didn't say much as he drove us through the parking lot and onto the surface road. I knew our destination without asking. For some reason, we always gravitated toward Miss Odilia's Southern Eatery whenever we had a chance to break for lunch. There was no telling when the habit started, but neither of us wanted to stop it now.

Within a few minutes, we arrived at the last curve before the restaurant. Someone had parked a pickup half-in and half-out of a pull-through driveway right before the restaurant's parking lot. The driver's maneuver forced Ambrose to swerve around the truck's bumper.

He jerked the wheel left. "Oh, crap!"

I stared at the offending truck as we drove past, since its profile looked awfully familiar. Sure enough, the Ford dually was the same one I'd seen at Dogwood Manor—the one that'd whisked Shep Truitt to the ER after he'd smashed his hand. Not only that, but the ponytailed driver who crouched on the truck's lowered guardrail looked exactly like Cole Truitt.

The truck hulked in the driveway of Uncle Billy's Self-Storage. The one-story brick building wore an orange roof, and it had a line of matching orange garage doors that fronted the road. The last storage unit on the left stood open, the yawning chasm like a missing fence post in a line of tangerine boards.

Apparently, Cole was busy arranging things in the bed of his truck, and he pushed aside a pile of shutters to make room for something else.

"Hey, Ambrose. Stop here." I leveled my gaze at the man by the truck bed.

"What for?"

"Just, please stop."

He didn't probe for a reason. Instead, he carefully pulled the Audi to the side of the road and slid the gearshift into Park. "What's going on, Missy? We're almost at the restaurant. I don't know about you, but I'm starving."

"Um-hum." I wasn't listening, though, since the activity in the truck bed mesmerized me. Cole had found a stained-glass window in the pile of shutters, which he carefully dislodged from the debris. The pink-and-green glass glistened in the midday sun. "That's Cole Truitt," I said.

"Cole who?"

Finally, I brought my gaze back to Ambrose. "That's Shep Truitt's son. The one who helped me out on Monday. I wonder what he's doing here."

"He's probably filling up a storage unit. Does it really matter?"

"It might."

At that moment, Cole placed the window on a quilted pad and carefully slid it to the ground, using the lowered guardrail for leverage.

"Do you mind if we go back there so I can talk to him?" I asked.

Ambrose looked askance. "Now? Can't you do it after lunch?"

I shook my head. "He'll be gone by then, I just know it. Please?"

"Okay." Ambrose didn't seem too happy with my request, but he put the car in Drive and pulled back onto the road. After making a U-turn, he returned to the self-storage facility and maneuvered the Audi alongside the pickup. We barely slid past the truck, with only five inches of space to spare between the two vehicles.

Once safely beyond the pickup, Ambrose parked in front of the manager's office, a squat stand-alone building with a neon OPEN sign flashing in the window.

"We're here," he said. "Now what?"

"Follow me." I hopped out of the car and made my way to the Ford. Thank goodness I was done posing for the magazine's photographer, because humidity seeped under my makeup the minute I stepped on the asphalt. I could only imagine what my shiny lip gloss and liquid foundation looked like by now.

Cole didn't seem to notice my arrival; he was too busy pulling things into the gap left by the stained-glass window.

He wore a New Orleans Baby Cakes gimme cap and a navy T-shirt, and sweat plastered the shirt to his back.

"Hello," I said once I reached him.

He started at the sound of my voice, before quickly turning. "Uh, hi."

"We were just driving down the road when we saw your truck." I tried to keep my tone light; no need to put him on the defensive. "Did I ever thank you for finding me a water bottle at Dogwood Manor?"

It was a lame way to start the conversation, and we both knew it.

"Uh...I don't remember. I think so."

I threw him a smile, which I hoped looked more genuine than it felt. "And then you helped me carry some supplies back to my studio. That was very nice of you. I really appreciate your thoughtfulness."

"*Oookkkaaayyy.* You're welcome. I guess." He indicated the pile in his truck bed with a sweep of his hand. In addition to the window, he'd stacked chipped shutters, pieces of crown molding, and a few marble pedestals in the truck bed. "I'm kinda busy here."

"I can see that. What's all this stuff?"

He returned his attention to the pile instead of answering me. Ambrose must have noticed the snub, because he quickly moved up beside me and extended his hand.

"Hey there. I'm Ambrose Jackson. Can I help you with all of this stuff?"

Cole stopped appraising the pile. "Man, that'd be great." He quickly rubbed his palm on his T-shirt and returned the handshake, his tone much warmer now. "I thought this stuff would be a lot lighter than it is. Guess I overestimated my strength."

Meanwhile, I subtly backed away from the two men. While I wanted to keep the conversation going, my white pantsuit had suffered more than its fair share of trauma today, and I wasn't sure it could handle any more. I'd have to ask my questions from a safe distance away.

"All of this wood looks really old," I said. "Especially the paint on the shutters. Did it all come from a construction site?"

"You could say that." Cole turned to Ambrose. "Let's lift on three. One...two...three."

The men hoisted the pile of shutters above their heads, then walked them away from the truck bed.

"Which construction site?" I hurried to catch up with them. At this point, I didn't care if Cole thought I was crazy, nosy, or a pain in the ass. I'd seen the same shutters in the back of his father's truck, so I knew they came from Dogwood Manor.

"I'm helping my dad out," he said. "Pop got them out of the trash at Mr. Solomon's place."

So the two men's stories *did* match. But what if both were lying? "Your dad got that window out of the trash? It seems awfully nice for someone to throw it away." I gazed toward the glass, which was propped against the side of the truck.

A similar window had hung in the foyer at Dogwood Manor. Three images marked it: a delicate flower with translucent petals; a silver chalice, flat and dull; and a green fleur-de-lis. The pink dogwood blossom, which was rimmed in red, stood out particularly well against the aqua background.

"It has a crack," he said. "Look at the bottom corner. You can barely see it now, but it's pretty obvious when there's light coming through it."

"That's a shame," Ambrose said. "So, what does your dad do with all this stuff?"

"He sells it online." Cole's gaze drifted to the pile of shutters again. "He figures he might as well get something out of that job he did for Herbert Solomon."

A memory came rushing back: Cole and I had stood in the parking lot behind my studio, our arms full of supplies from Homestyle Hardware. His paint can hit the pavement when he railed against Herbert Solomon and how the man had treated his father.

"You told me about that," I said. "Didn't Mr. Solomon try to cheat your dad out of some money?"

Instead of launching into another tirade, which I fully expected, Cole flinched. "Yeah…about that. I shouldn't have gone off about Mr. Solomon like that. He wasn't such a bad guy."

Wasn't a bad guy? Earlier, Cole had made it sound like he was angry enough to go after Mr. Solomon himself, which he would've done if the man wasn't already dead.

"I mean, look." The change in Cole's demeanor was striking. He'd gone from irritated to contrite in a matter of seconds. "The guy wasn't *that* bad. He wasn't the perfect employer, but I'm sure there are a lot worse."

I threw Ambrose a look. This new attitude was downright unnerving. If I didn't know better, I'd say Cole Truitt had an evil twin. One twin thought Mr. Solomon deserved every bad thing that ever happened to him, while this new, improved version was ready to forgive him on the spot.

"Wow," I said. "You've really changed your mind about him. What happened?"

"I dunno." He shrugged. "No use getting bitter about the past. By the way, that detective who came around the mansion said he knows you. Said you two grew up together. You never told me that before."

Aha. No wonder Cole had changed his tune. Now that he knew about my friendship with Lance, he didn't want to say or do anything that would make me suspicious of him.

"So Lance told you about that?" Now it was my turn to be evasive, since I had nothing to gain by being forthright. "Yeah, I guess I know him."

"That's not what he said." Obviously, the tables had turned, and Cole's eyes blazed with curiosity. "He said you two lived on the same street when you were growing up. You were neighbors, even. What a coincidence you both ended up here in Bleu Bayou."

Ambrose must have noticed when I blanched, because he placed his hand on my shoulder.

"I'm afraid it's time for us to leave, Cole. Can I help you move some of that other stuff?"

"Nah." Cole waved away the offer. "It's not that heavy. The shutters were the hardest part. If you'll just help me move those inside the unit, I can take it from there."

Together, the men lifted the pile of shutters from the ground and hoisted them waist-high this time. They quickly transferred the pile from the doorway of the unit to a far corner.

I tagged along behind them.

"That'll do it," Ambrose said. "You've got a huge unit here. It has to be, what? Fifteen, twenty feet?"

Cole nodded. "The biggest one they have. It's ten by twenty, to be exact."

All that room, for so few items. Could it be that Shep Truitt intended to "salvage" a lot more from Dogwood Manor?

"Guess it's time to go." Ambrose dusted his hands on the sides of his slacks.

"It was nice to see you again, Cole," I lied.

In fact, our visit with him left me feeling terribly unsettled. His attitude had changed so quickly, as if he wanted to rewrite our conversations in the past.

"You, too," he said. "See you around."

I left him by the pile of weathered shutters in the storage unit, my thoughts a million miles away. I barely noticed when Ambrose opened the car door for me. Instead, I absentmindedly slid onto the passenger seat and locked the seat belt in place.

"That was interesting," Ambrose said, once he hopped into the car, too.

"Mmmm."

"You okay?" His hand stalled over the ignition. "You seem preoccupied."

I snapped out of it just as he fired up the car. "That was so strange. Cole acted like he knew Lance and I were good friends all along, and for some reason, it bothered him. But why? Why would he care what I think about that...unless he has something to hide?"

"Good point." Ambrose pulled the car away from the storage facility and drove onto the road. "Maybe he doesn't want you to think he had anything to do with Solomon's death."

He made a hard right when we reached the restaurant, where we joined a line of cars waiting to enter the parking lot. Once inside, we found a spot in the very back row, sandwiched between a telephone pole and a Cadillac Escalade. He parked the car, and then we both stepped onto the hot asphalt.

The *crunch* of tires grinding into asphalt sounded all around me, along with the *screech* of metal doors opening and closing. I hurried onto the sidewalk in front of the restaurant, the back of my jacket already moist from the humidity.

Despite the heat, Miss Odilia somehow had managed to keep a half-dozen flowers alive in purple boxes that lined the restaurant's wall. In addition to red and pink zinnias, she'd carefully cultivated some foxglove plants, and the lavender stalks towered over their squatter neighbors.

Before Ambrose could usher me through the front door, the panel whipped open to reveal a man in a black-and-fuchsia Hawaiian shirt and khaki cargo pants. It was Hank Dupre, and he nearly bowled me over in his hurry to leave the restaurant.

"Whoa!" he said, as his shoulder banged into mine. "Pardon me."

"Hello, Hank."

He did a double take. "Hi, Missy. I didn't realize it was you."

"No problem."

Someone's head popped around Hank's shoulder just then. "Who's out there?"

"It's Missy DuBois," Hank said. "Nearly knocked her off the steps, I'm afraid. Can you back up a bit?"

The woman behind him retreated into the restaurant, and we all shuffled into the foyer. The female voice belonged to Waunzy Boudin, the town's historian and self-described remodeling addict.

"Hello, Miss Boudin," I said. "What a nice surprise."

Today, the elderly woman wore a bright yellow sundress, which she'd paired with lemon-colored flip-flops and a green parasol. "My word, it seems everyone in town goes to this restaurant. So nice to see you again, Missy."

"Do you know Ambrose?" I gestured in his direction.

"I do, indeed," she said. "How are you, Mr. Jackson?"

"Good. How was your lunch?"

Waunzy shot Hank a look. "It was only fair to middlin', I'm afraid. Odilia might be cutting some corners now that she owns two restaurants." She leaned closer. "Truth be told, my chicken tasted like it was cooked with Shake 'n Bake."

"Now, Waunzy." Hank frowned. "You know that's not possible. Maybe you just got a bad piece or two."

"Thank goodness it wasn't a total loss, though. Hank here has been sharing his real-estate knowledge with me. He's a font of information, you know."

"Why, you're not thinking of selling your house, are you?" I asked.

"I'm exploring the possibility. Might as well find out what I need to do to get the ball rolling."

"So, you *are* thinking of moving," I said.

"Here's the deal." She leaned even closer. "It's no secret I've had my eye on that lovely Dogwood Manor for years now."

"Waunzy," Hank cautioned. "You promised you wouldn't say anything."

"Oh, Hank." She quickly rolled her eyes. "You need to lighten up. Hank here's just worried the property won't come on the market after all, and I'll get disappointed. He thinks people will fight over that property and keep it tied up in the courts."

"Is that so?" I said. "I thought Ivy Solomon would automatically get it."

"Not necessarily." Hank met my gaze head-on. "There might be a prenuptial agreement that bequeaths it to another heir. No one knows for sure, and I didn't write up Herbert's will."

In addition to selling real estate around town, Hank had graduated with a law degree from LSU in the seventies. A lot of longtime residents still turned to him for help with wills, contracts, estate planning, and whatnot.

"Hmmm. There's only one problem," I said. "Mr. Solomon's only heir was his daughter, Trinity, but she passed away more than two years ago."

"That's true," Hank said. "But he might've left it to a university, or another charity, or a sibling, even. We'll have to see."

"I'm sure it'll all work out," Waunzy said. "There's no reason to think the house won't go on the market, and I'll be the first one in line when it does…you can count on that."

"Isn't that house a little big for just one person?" Finally, Ambrose got a word in edgewise. "I don't mean to be disrespectful, ma'am, but that's a lot of house for one person to maintain."

"Why, Mr. Jackson." Waunzy was clearly warming up to the topic, since her eyes shone. "What makes you think I want to maintain that place all on my own? I might have other plans for it. A surprise, if you will."

"You're going to turn it into a B&B," I guessed. "Aren't you?"

"Maybe," she said. "Maybe not. Y'all will just have to wait and see. Speaking of which, I probably should get going. I forgot some things at the hardware store yesterday. No time like the present."

With that, she sashayed past us and paused by the exit. "Are you coming, Hank? Time's a-wastin'."

Hank shrugged and stepped over the threshold, while she held the door open for him.

"Will you look at those zinnias!" She paused on the first step. "My, my. That Odilia does know her way around a flower box. 'Course, that crabgrass on the sidewalk is another story."

Ambrose shifted next to me, since he was ready to eat, I supposed. But I didn't move. Curiosity kept me rooted to the spot, since Waunzy still held the door open for Hank. *Maybe she'll mention Dogwood Manor again.*

"Look," Waunzy said, as she pointed at something. "That crabgrass should be pulled up by its roots. How much do you want to bet Odilia uses that smelly MSMA instead?"

Finally, she released her grip on the door, and it slowly inched closed. I could still hear her voice through the gap, though, which kept me rooted to the spot.

"No doubt," she said. "She'll knock it out with chemicals instead of getting down on her hands and knees."

Once the door banged shut, I completely lost track of Waunzy and Hank.

"What's wrong?" Ambrose asked. "You look like you've seen a ghost."

"Did you hear that? Did you listen to her talk about the crabgrass outside?"

"Not really. Why?"

"She knew the trade name for crabgrass poison." Waunzy's words echoed around me, as if she'd just spoken. "Don't you think that's a little strange?"

"Maybe she learned it at the hardware store."

"Maybe." I moved closer to him, although no one else could hear us. "You don't usually get that poison at the hardware store, though. It's a professional product."

"I still don't understand what you're getting at, and my stomach is starting to growl."

"Ambrose Jackson." I stressed his name, willing him to understand. "Put your stomach on hold for a moment. MSMA is a compound with arsenic."

"Now, how would *you* know something like that?"

"Because my assistant went to pharmacy school, remember? Beatrice told me about it when I found some weeds out in front of the studio. But it's also something people use as a poison."

"She said that?" he asked.

"Yep. And that's the same poison that killed Herbert Solomon."

"Okay, maybe you're right. That *is* a little weird."

"It's not only weird, it's downright uncanny." I tried to recall Waunzy's exact words. "She definitely said Odilia would use that 'smelly MSMA,' instead of pulling out the weeds by hand. She seemed very familiar with the chemical."

After a second, Ambrose groaned. "Let me guess…we're not going to eat lunch now, are we?"

"Huh?"

"You're going to chase down Detective LaPorte and forget all about our lunch."

This man knows me too well. Although, to my everlasting credit, I almost changed my mind when I saw the look on his face.

"I'm sorry, Bo. I really am. But you heard her. Not to mention, I ran into Cole at the hardware store, too, only he was picking up a different product with arsenic. The coincidences keep piling up, and I can't wait anymore to let Lance know about them. As Waunzy said, 'Time's a-wastin'.'"

CHAPTER 19

By the time Waunzy and Hank disappeared down the sidewalk, another pair of diners had taken their place by the entrance, and they barreled through the door.

One of the men wore a gold LSU Tigers' T-shirt with a Pelicans' ball cap, as if he couldn't decide between the two sports teams, while his buddy wore a "Who Dat?" jersey and a matching cap that left no question as to *his* loyalty.

The Saints fan slapped his friend on the back, then they both moved into the restaurant.

"Look, I can't call Lance from here," I whispered. "There's too much going on. Mind if I call him from your car?"

"No, of course not." Ambrose reached into his pants pocket and withdrew his keys. "Just keep the air conditioner on, or you'll burn up out there."

"Deal." Although it wasn't the best option, it was the only one I had. "You go ahead and grab a table. I don't mind."

"No," he said. "On second thought…I'll go with you. There's no use for you to sit outside in the parking lot all by yourself."

We made our way to the exit and walked down the steps. At that moment, a large silver sedan pulled into the lot, with its right blinker on. I only noticed the car because sunshine ricocheted off the amber light and nearly blinded me.

I cupped my hand over my eyes, and that's when I spied the car's hood, where a shiny statue of a winged nymph looked ready to dive off the slick grille.

"Sweet mother-of-pearl," I whispered. "Look who's here."

I pointed at the Rolls-Royce, which slowly cruised down the aisle, headed straight for us. The woman behind the wheel sported the same trendy, asymmetrical haircut and oversized sunglasses as always.

"Who's that?" Ambrose asked.

"I don't know for sure. But if I had to guess, I'd say it's Mr. Solomon's girlfriend."

Without thinking, I automatically jogged forward to flag her down, since I wasn't about to let her disappear for the third time. Somehow, she didn't see me, or more likely, she pretended she couldn't see me.

"Here, let me." Ambrose strode into the path of the oncoming car and firmly crossed his arms, which left the driver only two options: She could either stop, or she could swerve around him and crash that expensive hood ornament into one of the neighboring cars.

She finally tapped the brakes and stuck her head out the window as the Rolls shuddered to a stop. "Yes? What do you want?"

I moved over to the driver's side, which still was missing its mirror, of course. "Hi there. It's nice to see you again."

"Look. Do I know you?" she asked.

I couldn't read her eyes behind the dark sunglasses, but she sounded peeved. "You asked me for directions on Monday. Did you ever find the interstate?"

"Excuse me?"

"You asked me about the interstate," I prodded. "You missed the on-ramp for it, and you were lost."

"That's right." Finally, she pulled off the oversized glasses and tossed them onto the dash. She had classically beautiful features—upturned eyes with long, thick lashes; a delicate, heart-shaped face; and a small cleft in the middle of her chin.

"Sorry. I thought you were someone else I ran into yesterday."

Ambrose joined me at the window. "Wow, what a great car! I used to know a guy who owned one just like this."

"I highly doubt it. They're not very common around here." She spoke without looking at him.

"No, I'm pretty certain he had a Silver Shadow, too."

When she finally glanced up at Ambrose, she did a quick double take. "Oh my. Is that so? Not too many people around here drive one of these. Thank you for the compliment." She batted her lush eyelashes at him.

Is she flirting with him? "Anyhoo, what a coincidence to run into you here," I said.

"I'll say." She offered Ambrose her hand. "I'm Evangeline. And you're…"

"Ambrose. Ambrose Jackson." He gamely took the hand she offered. "And this is Melissa DuBois."

"We met on Monday," I reminded her, hoping she'd forget all about our little interaction yesterday. "This is such a beautiful car. Is it yours?"

"Of course it's mine." Her gaze remained locked on Ambrose. "The engine purrs like a kitten. And the upholstery...well, it feels like butter. Have you ever driven one?"

"Can't say I have," he answered. "But I used to know someone who owned one just like it. He was a property developer."

She blinked, but this time it wasn't flirtatious. "Why, you must be talking about Herbert. Herbert Solomon."

"That's him," he said. "Did you know him?"

"I did, as a matter of fact. Well, I've got to get going. It's about a million degrees outside, and y'all must be burning up."

"We're fine," I lied. In reality, humidity pressed my suit jacket flat and made it hard to breathe. "How did you happen to get Mr. Solomon's car?"

She reached for the sunglasses. "Not that it's any of your business... but he gave it to me." By now, her phony politeness had worn thin. "If you don't mind, I'm in a hurry."

She moved again, but this time she reached for a button to close the window.

"Don't go!"

The car lurched forward as Evangeline floored the accelerator. The Rolls sped away in a cloud of road dust and pea gravel, its whitewall tires blurred by the haze.

I turned to Ambrose. "We've got to follow her!"

Luckily, he was one step ahead of me. "C'mon," he yelled over his left shoulder, as he sprinted toward the Audi.

I followed, doing my best to run in the stiff business suit. By the time I pulled up next to him, the pants encased my legs like a wet, clammy blanket.

I threw open the passenger door and slid onto the seat as Ambrose drove the car away from the parking lot. In no time flat, we'd pulled up behind the Rolls.

"She's going to get us killed," Ambrose said, as the fancy car careened through an intersection without slowing. "Remind me again why we're doing this."

"Because Lance will want to talk to her. I mean, c'mon...this can't be legit." I spied the outline of the Factory up ahead, but it whizzed past in a blur of red bricks and tin roof. "And I think I know where she's going. It looks like she's headed for Dogwood Manor."

"Hold on!"

Ambrose accelerated the car until it touched the Rolls' bumper. A pair of shocked eyes appeared in the rearview mirror ahead of us, Evangeline's glances becoming more and more furtive as the two cars raced down Church Street.

After tailgating a moment longer, Ambrose swerved left, prepared to pass her on the two-lane road.

"Wait a minute," I said. "She'll turn right here."

Sure enough, the chain-link fence around Dogwood Manor appeared up ahead. Evangeline checked her rearview mirror one last time, then she swerved through the mansion's wrought-iron gate. She finally skidded to a stop by the marble steps.

She hopped out of the car as I wrenched open the door of the Audi.

"What's wrong with you?" she yelled.

"Me?" I carefully stepped toward her, since we'd already spooked her once today. "We just want to talk to you. We know who you are."

"You do?"

"Of course we do. You're Herbert Solomon's girlfriend." I kept my voice neutral, since it wouldn't do a lick of good to judge the woman at this point. While I didn't approve of cheating spouses and illicit affairs, her love life was really none of my business. The same couldn't be said of Herbert Solomon's death, though, since *that* had become my business the moment I stumbled across his body in the back bedroom.

Ambrose joined us by the kudzu-encased steps. "Thank goodness you stopped."

"You could've gotten us killed back there," she said. The flirtatious tone was gone. "Why would you try to pass me like that?"

"Because I was afraid you were going to run another stop sign," he said.

"She's not the best driver," I mumbled under my breath.

"Look, I shouldn't even be here." The woman quickly glanced at the mansion. "I really don't want to cause any trouble."

It's a little too late for that. "What're you doing here, then?" I asked.

"I forgot something inside."

I glanced at the house, too, which seemed so lonely now. Strips of yellow caution tape crisscrossed over the blue tarp like leftover sticks from the Tinkertoy set, and the tools once more lay idle. Even the cicadas refused to sing without an audience. "You can't go in there. I bet the police took everything back to the station, anyway."

"Not everything," she said. "I left something behind in our bedroom."

I blanched, since the mere thought of Herbert Solomon in bed gave me the heebie-jeebies. It was hard to believe that this woman—or any woman—would want to be intimate with him, especially since Evangeline was twice as attractive as him and only half his age.

"Well, you'll just have to tell the police about it," I said.

"Speaking of which"—Ambrose lowered his phone to his side—"they should be here any minute. I called Lance and told him about the Rolls-Royce."

Sure enough, the dusty hood of a police cruiser pulled onto the property a few moments later. I'd have to compliment Ambrose on his speed-dialing as soon as the dust settled.

"Thank goodness," I whispered, as the cruiser pulled up to the Rolls.

Instead of parking beside the sedan, though, Lance reversed course and fishtailed the back end of his cruiser to block the Silver Shadow from leaving. He quickly popped out from behind the wheel and marched over to us.

"Are you Evangeline Roy?" he asked, once he'd arrived.

It was an accusation, not a question, and the woman meekly nodded.

"We've been looking for you," he said. "You'll have to come with me."

"Do…do you have a warrant?" she stammered, as if cowed by the police uniform and the gun at Lance's side. "I thought you had to have a warrant before you could take me anywhere."

"Nice try, but you're wrong." He reached into his shirt pocket and pulled out a sheet of paper. "I got one anyway, though, just to be safe. The magistrate judge signed it this morning."

She glumly read the sheet he passed to her. "All right, I'll go with you. But I forgot something in the mansion and I'm going to need it. Can I please run inside for a minute? Please."

"What is it?" Lance asked.

"My credit card. Herbert threatened to cut it up, because he thought I spent too much money on clothes. He wanted to 'set a good example'." She quickly flicked her first and second fingers up and down to indicate quote marks. "I told him I already threw the card away, but I really hid it in the bedroom."

"We'll probably need that for evidence," Lance said. "So, the answer's no."

"But it's mine." She sounded desperate now. "It's my personal property. You can't keep it for no reason."

"Look…I'm investigating a possible felony, so I can keep anything I want. Especially if it pertains to the case."

"But Herbert never used the card, and he didn't even know I had it anymore." Her gaze dropped to the ground. "I don't have a penny on me. What if I need to hire an attorney?"

Lance thought it over. "Okay. I'm going to let you retrieve it, but you can only keep it if it's in your name. If it belongs to Herbert Solomon, it goes straight to the evidence room."

"It *was* mine. I promise." She brought her gaze back to his face, her eyes suddenly hopeful. "An Amex. I got it for my hair salon, but I kinda used it for other stuff."

"I'll tell you what." Lance spoke to me and Ambrose now. "I'll go inside and look for the lady's card. You two watch her out here." He reached for a pair of shiny handcuffs that were tucked into the waistband of his slacks. "She won't be able to go anywhere with these on."

"You don't have to handcuff me," Evangeline said.

"Let's just call it extra insurance." Lance quickly wrapped the cuffs around her wrists and snapped the lock closed. "You said your card's in the bedroom?"

"That's right. Near the library. I hid it under the mattress when he wasn't looking."

"Back in a minute."

Lance quickly headed up the stairs, then disappeared under the blue tarp. No one spoke for the longest time, and when we did, we all asked the same question: What was taking Lance so long?

CHAPTER 20

An uncomfortable silence fell over us. Part of me felt sorry for Evangeline Roy, since sweat trickled down her cheeks unchecked, but another part felt irritated, since she'd put us all at risk when she careened down Church Street. Not to mention, she'd run a red light when I'd tried to follow her the day before.

And last but not least, she'd taken up with a married man, although I'd vowed not to judge her about her personal life.

The judgment would come later, when people in town got wind of her affair with Herbert Solomon. He wasn't well-liked to begin with, and this would put everyone over the top. Since they couldn't ostracize *him* anymore, they'd probably turn on his girlfriend instead.

The silence continued. When a good five minutes had come and gone, and Lance still wasn't back, I turned to Ambrose. "What do you think happened to him?"

"Give him some time. Maybe he ran across something else he needs to take back to the police station."

"Maybe." I began to chew my lower lip. "He could've called me, you know. He doesn't usually disappear like this."

"If he doesn't come out soon, we'll go in after him."

The next five minutes dragged on and on. Although Evangeline finally wiped her sweaty cheeks on the sleeve of her blouse, we all felt miserable. Ambrose shifted from one foot to the next, while I tried—unsuccessfully—to work up a breeze by fanning my face with my hand.

"What about now?" I asked, when another few minutes had passed.

"Okay," he said. "But I want Evangeline to go in first."

She motioned to the uneven walkway with her shackled wrists. "But what if I fall?"

"It's okay," he said. "We'll steady you. C'mon."

He took hold of her shoulder and nudged her forward. She took one tentative step, then another.

By the time she disappeared under the blue tarp, I was right behind the two of them. While everything in the shadowy foyer looked the same—a brass chandelier still dangled from the domed ceiling, smooth plaster covered the walls, and mahogany stairs curved to the second floor—small differences soon appeared.

The light switch by the front door looked dirtier now. Something black had smudged the plastic plate, as if inky fingers had rubbed against the surface. When I did a double take, I realized the "grime" was really carbon powder, designed to highlight fingerprints on a white surface.

A different powder dusted the wood stair rail. Here, an investigator used white powder—probably a mix of titanium and oxide—to contrast with the deep red wood.

I'd learned about fingerprint powders when I'd helped Lance solve Trinity Solomon's murder. He'd allowed me to analyze her bedroom, which was dusted with several different powders, depending on the color and texture of the object in question. The white wooden door to her bedroom required a black powder, for instance, while the iron doorknob on it called for a neutral coat of silver.

Speaking of which…even the ground of the foyer looked different now. When I'd first arrived at the mansion Monday, a thin layer of sawdust had coated the floor. Since that time, someone had swirled a circular pattern in the dust.

Curious, I slid over to the staircase and climbed a few steps to get a bird's-eye view.

Someone had created a pattern in the sawdust. It looked like "the wheel" Lance had told me about. He'd said investigators paced in ever-widening circles when they wanted to study a room. The result was a swirling pattern that looked like something a monk would rake in the pebbles of a Zen garden.

I shook my head, and the image vanished.

"Are you coming, Missy?" Ambrose stood to one side of the foyer, as if deciding which hall to enter.

"Just a second!" I hopped to the floor and hurried to catch up with him. "We need to go down the east hall. That's where Solomon's bedroom was."

There was still no sign of Lance. As we made our way down the windowless hall, our path brightened by a few wall sconces placed here and there, I noticed the closed doors on either side. Every door was shut tight, except for the last door on the left, where a dull, yellow glow spilled onto the drop cloth.

"There it is," I said. "The last room before the library. That's where I found Mr. Solomon's body on Monday."

Ambrose stepped in front of Evangeline. The doorway was crisscrossed with crime-scene tape, just like the front entrance. I glanced over his shoulder to peer into the murky room.

The saw-toothed outline of packing boxes appeared first, minus the dusty sheets that had covered them earlier. The cardboard boxes wore shipping labels filled with black ink in spidery handwriting. Now that I had time to study the words, the handwriting looked like it belonged to Mr. Solomon, judging by the purchase order I'd watched him sign for Erika Daniels in the library earlier.

Behind the boxes lay the piece of furniture I'd wondered about. It was a dresser, after all, and it matched the ornately carved canopy bed.

"I don't know if I can go in there again," I whispered to Ambrose. "It feels so strange to be back in his bedroom."

"It's okay," Ambrose said. "You don't have to go inside. Wait here."

He reached for the crime-scene tape and pulled it from the doorjamb. Once the plastic fell free, he stepped into the room.

"Wait a second." I gently nudged Evangeline forward, and then I followed her into the room. I had no intention of leaving her in the hall by herself, just as I had no intention of being away from Ambrose. "I'd rather be in here with you."

"Atta girl," Ambrose said.

I cautiously approached the canopied bed. The *Bleu Bayou Impartial Reporter* was gone, as was the glass finial I'd knocked from the headboard. Someone had removed the bedsheets from the mattress, too, which exposed a blue-ticked surface.

Unlike the elegant bedroom upstairs, this room was cramped and musty. Maybe Mr. Solomon never noticed it, since everyone told me he worked twenty-four hours a day. And Evangeline probably didn't care, as long as he'd gifted her with a Rolls-Royce and who knew what else.

At that moment, something sounded behind me, and I nearly tripped onto the bed.

"There you are," a voice called out.

I swirled around to see Lance, his navy uniform a dark blot against the hall light.

"Lance!" I almost crumbled onto the bed anyway, before I thought better of it. No need to mess up a crime scene that was part of an active investigation. "Where the heck did you go? You had us worried sick."

"Sorry about that." He nodded at something over his shoulder. "I found someone else walking around the property, so I had to take care of first things first. It looks like I caught myself a trespasser."

When he stepped aside, another figure appeared in the doorway, only this one wasn't nearly as tall, or as wide, as Lance. It was Waunzy Boudin, and her bright yellow sundress practically glowed in the gloomy hall.

"Dear me," she said. "Am I in trouble?"

I gawked at the newest addition to our party. "What in the world are you doing here, Miss Boudin?"

When she didn't respond, I turned to Lance for an explanation. "She wasn't really trespassing, was she?"

"I'm afraid so." He stepped into the room. "She was in the kitchen with some cans of paint. Caught her using a paper towel to wipe some on the wall."

Waunzy shrugged, as if she didn't understand what all the fuss was about. "I didn't mean any harm. I thought I'd have a little fun with the colors in the kitchen. I wanted to see what the different shades looked like on the wall. Just in case, you know."

"That's no excuse," I said. "You know better than to come inside an active crime scene."

"I honestly didn't think anyone would mind," she said. "It's not like I planned to steal anything. I just wanted to see whether my hunch about the colors was right."

"It doesn't matter," Lance said. "You'll have to leave now."

"Of course, Officer. Whatever you say." Waunzy turned to go. Before she got very far, though, something else caught her attention. "What in the world…"

She stepped forward before anyone else could move. When she reached the dresser, she leaned over it to study the wall.

"Miss Boudin!" Lance tried to follow her, but too many people stood in his way.

Waunzy didn't appear to hear him. She was too busy studying the wall in front of her.

"What's wrong?" I asked.

She didn't respond to me, either, so I followed her gaze to the wall. It was papered in an emerald pattern of vines and leaves that grew toward the ceiling. Granted, the green color was awfully vibrant, considering the background had faded to mush. Waunzy studied the paper for a good minute, as if the leaves were made of actual emeralds.

"This is amazing," she said.

"What is?" Lance asked.

"I haven't seen this in years. Years. The last time I did, it was in a museum."

Evangeline sighed heavily. "Look, this is interesting and all, but I really need that credit card. Can't we just get it and go?"

"Shhhh." Lance made a slashing motion with his hand. "Let the lady speak. What did you see in a museum, Miss Boudin?"

"This." She pointed to a green vine, her finger trembling. "This is antique wallpaper. It dates back to the eighteen fifties, at least."

"Again, this is interesting and all," Evangeline began, "but I don't see..."

"Shhh!" This time, we all turned to silence her.

Once I'd helped shush Evangeline, I returned my gaze to the wallpaper. Small gaps appeared between the brightly colored panels, and the upper edge curled away from the crown molding like a tiny wave. Every so often, a water stain appeared in the background. It looked like every other wallpaper I'd seen in the antebellum homes around here, although none of the others boasted a green that was quite so vibrant.

Usually, the papers featured flowers—everyday ones, like sunflowers or daisies, in the casual rooms, and fancier varieties, like roses or lilies, in formal spaces—and the primary colors ran to pinks, reds, and yellows.

"I don't understand," I said.

Several things in the bedroom—including the canopy bed and brass gasolier—were antiques, but no one had questioned *them*. "Why does that make a difference?"

"You don't know, do you?" Waunzy's voice was soft. "For a while, this green color was all the rage in Victorian England. They used it to dye their paints, their wallpapers...even their ballgowns, for goodness sakes. They called it Scheel's Green, or sometimes Paris Green. No one thought twice about it, until people started to get sick."

"Wait a minute," Lance said. "If it was made in England, how did it end up here, in Bleu Bayou?"

"Even I know that one," I said. "The man who built this house came from London. Miss Boudin told me he brought over cargo boxes filled with fabrics and accessories to decorate his beautiful new mansion."

"That's right." She seemed pleased to know I'd been listening. "He probably thought this wallpaper would impress everyone, because he didn't know what the paper was made of."

"Well, what is it made of?" Ambrose asked.

"Arsenic." Her tone was matter-of-fact. "The manufacturer called it Paris Green. All the rich people had to have it. But eventually people started to notice something strange. Their children got sick first, and then their servants, because their workers couldn't afford a healthy diet and their immune systems were compromised."

I gawked at her. "That makes perfect sense! Cole Truitt told me all about Mr. Solomon's junk-food diet during the renovation. He said the old man lived on Totino's Pizza Rolls and Diet Coke!"

Lance looked confused, so I quickly explained. "You remember Cole... his dad was the construction foreman at Dogwood Manor. He said Mr. Solomon wouldn't eat anything healthy while he lived here." I returned my gaze to Waunzy. "Do you think that's what made him get sick. The wallpaper?"

"Probably," she said. "Since it was right by his bed, he would inhale the chemical every night."

"But what about Evangeline?" Ambrose turned to her. "Did you notice anything strange about this room?"

"Please." She rolled her eyes. "I told Herbert I'd spend as little time here as possible. I mean, look at this place. We would meet over at Morningside Plantation."

I groaned when she mentioned the other mansion. Unfortunately, Ivy Solomon, Herbert's widow, had taken up residence there once she came to Bleu Bayou to plan the man's funeral. Heaven only knows how Ivy would feel when she found out her husband had used the property for his tête-à-têtes.

"I'm afraid our Mr. Solomon was in good company." Waunzy once more studied the paper as she spoke. "Not a lot of people know this, but Napoleon probably died from arsenic poisoning, too, thanks to some wallpaper. He lived in a house on St. Helena—once the French banished him to the island—which was full of wallpaper made with Paris Green. The sicker he got, the more time he spent indoors. They used to think he died of stomach cancer, but now we know that arsenic probably killed him."

"So, let me get this straight." Lance gestured at the wallpaper. "This paper could've made Herbert Solomon sick enough to die from arsenic poisoning?"

"I know it sounds crazy," Waunzy admitted, "but yes. If someone inhales the chemical night after night, it builds up in their bloodstream. The lungs and kidneys go first. We know enough today to remove the paper, thank goodness. It's usually the first thing a decorator will do when she's working on a historic property."

"Did you say 'decorator'?" I shot Lance a look.

"Yes, if they have any kind of formal training," Waunzy said. "It's hard to miss, what with the green color. A woman—or man—would have to be blind not to notice it."

Lance met my gaze head-on. "Are you thinking what I'm thinking, Missy?"

"Definitely. I think it's time for you to find Erika Daniels."

CHAPTER 21

The next few moments passed in a blur. First, Lance withdrew a latex glove from his back pocket, which he slipped over his right hand. Then he walked to the canopied bed and carefully ran his fingers under the mattress. After a moment or two, he pulled something out from under the bedding and straightened.

"Got it." He held aloft a worn American Express card, which he flipped over and read. "Yep, it belongs to Miss Roy."

Evangeline gave a sigh of relief. "Thank goodness!"

"Not so fast." Lance walked over to where she stood. "I'm going to give this card to you," he said, as he unlocked the handcuffs and handed her the card, "but you'll need to go down to the police station right now and give a sworn statement. I'll have an officer meet you in front of the mansion. The Rolls-Royce needs to stay here for now."

"No problem." She happily accepted the card. "I'm just thrilled to have my Amex back."

"Remember…it's a sworn statement. You'll be under oath."

"Got it." Even Lance's dire warning couldn't dull Evangeline's mood, though, and she practically skipped from the room.

Next, Lance withdrew his cell phone and called for a backup unit. Once he clicked off the line, he began to take pictures of the wallpaper behind the dresser. He moved too close to it at one point for Waunzy's liking, and she reached out for his arm.

"Not so close." She gave a gentle tug. "There's no shelf life to arsenic. It stays toxic forever."

In the meantime, Ambrose and I looked around the room, trying to find more of the deadly wallpaper. Fortunately, every other wall wore a coat of dull eggshell-colored paint. Once we finished scouring the room, we returned to the canopy bed.

"Ironic, isn't it?" I asked.

"What's that?"

"Here, people thought this wallpaper was *sooo* cool. The guy who built Dogwood Manor shipped it all the way from England. I'll bet if you go back and look at the county records, they'll say he died of some mysterious illness."

Ambrose thought it over. "Actually, we don't know what this room used to be. Maybe it wasn't always a bedroom."

"True." I glanced again at the innocent-looking vines covering the wall. Delicate stalks tapered up and out and ended just shy of the ceiling. "Which only makes it sadder. It could've been a nursery, or maybe a library, where people spent hours reading books. It upsets me to think of all the people who touched this wall, without ever realizing it was poisonous."

"Then don't think about it," Ambrose said. "We have more important things to worry about right now."

Now that we'd scoured all the walls, we wandered back to Lance, who took a final photo before lowering his phone.

"I can take you to Erika Daniels," I said. "She has an office at the Factory."

"That's right," Ambrose said. "Missy here ran into her in the lobby on Monday. That's when they figured out they both rented studios at the Factory."

Now it was my turn to look pleased, since Ambrose had obviously been listening to me. "I can't believe you remembered that! It was right after I saw her at Dogwood Manor. To be honest, I felt sorry for Erika, because she'd just lost her job at the mansion."

"Look, we could stay here all day and discuss this," Lance said. "But it's time for us to get the murderer. And I should probably cover up this wall before I leave."

"That's true." Waunzy hovered nearby. "Even though it takes a while for the poison to build up in people's systems, it's quicker if they touch the wall and then lick a finger." She shuddered lightly. "You don't want that to happen to anyone."

"Gotcha." Lance checked his watch. "It's twelve thirty now. I'll leave a message for the responding officer that he has to seal up this room when he comes for Miss Roy."

"You know what I can't get over?" Waunzy had finally stopped studying the paper, and now her eyes held a faraway look. "I actually feel sorry for Herbert Solomon. I'm sure he never suspected a thing."

"Probably not," Lance agreed.

"That's something I thought would never happen." Waunzy *tsk*ed a few times. "Me feeling sorry for that old tightwad. Go figure."

With a final *cluck* of her tongue, Waunzy left the room and wandered into the hall, and we all followed suit.

Unlike the bedroom, the walls in the hall wore smooth white plaster, like vanilla frosting spread over an angel food cake.

I ran my hand along the nearest one. "Let's only hope the original owner used wallpaper in just one room and not the whole house."

"You're right." Ambrose spoke up behind me. "But anything could be under all this plaster. Guess the next owner will have to rip out the walls to be sure."

"Not necessarily." Unlike Ambrose and I, Waunzy didn't sound too concerned. "You should see the stacks of photos I have back at my office. Piles and piles of them. The Bleu Bayou Historical Society has more old pictures than you can shake a stick at. I can figure out which walls had wallpaper on them in no time at all. It'll be like figuring out a giant puzzle...and I do love a good puzzle."

Now it was Waunzy's turn to practically skip as she moved away from us and down the hall.

"Well, don't that beat all." I turned to address Lance, who stood beside me now. "Here I thought Waunzy would be devastated, since she wanted to buy this house and restore it."

"She doesn't look devastated to me," he said. "And there'll be time later to figure out who's going to get the mansion. Right now, we need to get the person responsible for killing Herbert Solomon. Are you coming with me, Missy?"

"Huh?"

"Do you want to be there when I interview Erika Daniels?" he asked.

My gaze flew to Ambrose, who, no doubt, would want me to say no, since he'd urged me to stay away from police investigations. "I dunno if I should go."

"You're the one who found the body," Lance said. "And you're the one who's helped me before. You don't even have to get out of the squad car. Just listen to what Erika Daniels has to say for herself."

"I know, I know." I tossed him a grin, against my better judgment. "You want me to use that 'freaky sixth-sense thing.' You want me to figure out if she's lying. What do you think, Ambrose?"

"It's okay," he said. "I really do trust your judgment. And it sounds like Lance needs you right now."

"Thanks, Bo." I wrapped my arms around him and squeezed for all I was worth. Amazing to think how far he'd come in only a few short days. Ambrose used to hate it when I helped Lance, but now he supported my decision. *If that's not progress, I don't know what is.*

CHAPTER 22

Lance and I left the hall soon afterward, too concerned with our mission to remain in place. Once we arrived in the foyer, the sound of an idling car engine broke our silence. The machine rumbled away on the other side of the plastic tarp, and staccato bursts of blue light swept under its hem.

"My backup got here so quick," Lance said.

I followed him under the tarp and onto the marble steps. The kudzu seemed even thicker now, since fewer people had tromped over it during the past few days, and roots brushed against my ankles.

After a quick glance at the responding officer, who sat in his squad car with Evangeline Roy, I threw open the door to Lance's dusty cruiser and slid onto the passenger seat.

Which wasn't easy, considering the inside of the car was a mess. Beside me lay a rumpled Cheetos bag and a week's supply of the *Bleu Bayou Impartial Reporter*. A crushed Dr Pepper can and some gum wrappers dirtied the floorboard around my feet.

"For goodness sake, Lance," I said, as I shoved the muck aside. "I don't know what's worse…your diet or your mess."

"You sound like my mom." He'd slipped behind the wheel and started the engine. Once he engaged the light bar on the car's roof, he quickly maneuvered the cruiser onto LA-18. "The only time I can find stuff is when it's like this."

I did my best to ignore the mess as we traveled to the Factory. As expected, every parking space was full, since lunch was over, but Lance drove straight ahead until we reached the glass door of the lobby, then he angled the car alongside the curb. It was the best spot in the lot.

"One of the benefits of being a cop." He killed the ignition and threw open the door. "Now, where's her office?"

"That's a good question." I tried to remember everything Erika Daniels had said when we'd met in the lobby. "I think it's on the second floor, close to Pink Cake Boxes."

"Got it." Lance exited the car and hopped onto the sidewalk.

When I did the same, he threw me a funny look. "You can stay in the car, you know."

"No way." Shards of sunlight ricocheted off the chrome bumpers and glass windshields all around me and warmed my body from head to toe. "For one thing, it's hotter than Hades out here. For another, I can just wait in the lobby while you take her into custody."

He nodded, and we stepped toward the entrance. The minute he threw open the plate-glass door, a wash of cold air hit me, which felt heavenly after sitting in the stifling police cruiser for the ride over.

"I'll wait right here." I strode over to a sleek Mies van der Rohe couch that anchored the lobby. I had the whole couch to myself, since the rest of the building was hard at work. Even the Starbucks barista was gone.

Normally, the woman works behind a counter tucked near the back wall. A line of customers usually zigzags across the lobby early in the morning, and it doesn't disappear until almost noon. But now, a silver roll-bar blocked the counter from the rest of the lobby, and the barista had swept every surface clean.

Lance quickly made his way to the elevator. He glanced around the empty space, then carefully withdrew a Glock 22 from his holster. When the elevator doors *whoosh*ed open, he leaned forward and prepared to enter.

Lorda mercy! Erika Daniels stood in the otherwise empty car with a shocked look on her face.

"That's her, Lance!" I screamed, as I moved away from the couch.

Everything slowed. Erika's gaze ricocheted from Lance to me and back again. When she realized what was happening, she suddenly lurched forward, which sent some papers in her hand flying into the air, like a snowstorm.

Lance leveled the Glock at her. "Stop right there."

He cocked the gun for good measure. Fortunately, the ploy worked, and Erika wobbled to a stop, her high heels *ping*ing against the sleek tile floor.

"What's...what's all this about?" Her gaze flew back to my face. "What'd you tell him, Missy?"

"Put your hands up," Lance said. "Now."

"Bu...but why?" She took a deep breath, then did as he'd asked. All the while, she looked to me for answers. "What did you *tell* him, Missy?" "Only the truth," I said. "That's all." Suddenly, her face hardened. "Don't listen to her, Officer. She's lying. Whatever she told you, don't believe it. She's trying to frame me." Lance didn't pay any attention to her, of course. "You have the right to remain silent..." Her gaze ping-ponged around the room. "She's...she's...she's trying to get even with me." She spoke quickly now, grasping at straws. "That's it. Missy owes me money. She can't pay me, so she's trying to get rid of me."

Lance continued to read Erika her rights as he expertly pulled another pair of handcuffs from his waistband. Then he slipped them around her wrists and engaged the lock, all while keeping the Glock trained on her face. A crisp *sssnnnaaapp* echoed in the lobby as the cuffs clicked shut.

"You have the right to speak to an attorney," he said, "and to have an attorney present during any questioning."

She obviously wasn't listening to him, because her expression fell flat. "Why didn't you stay out of it, Missy? Now look what you've done. I did us all a favor by getting rid of that horrible man. But you had to go and ruin it!"

"He had a wife, Erika," I said in a stage whisper, chilled by the blank look in her eyes. She only cared about herself; that much was obvious. "How can you live with yourself?"

"Me? That man was cheating on his lovely wife. Didn't you know? He was seeing some tramp on the side." She looked disgusted now, as if she couldn't believe Herbert Solomon's gall. "He even wanted me to create this beautiful bedroom for him and his lover on the second floor of the mansion. For that he'd spare no expense. *Pppffffttt.* But when it came to my fee? He tried to stiff me. Said I should be grateful for whatever pittance he gave me, because I was just starting out in the business. That's when I decided he didn't deserve to live."

"So, you shoved him into a tiny bedroom where you knew he'd breathe in poison night after night?" I asked. "That's just sick."

She smiled faintly. "Is it? Is it really? I thought the plan was quite ingenious. He never suspected that the reason I wanted him to sleep in that bedroom was because of the wallpaper. For once he trusted me and did just what I asked. The fool."

"Do you understand these rights..." Lance continued. He wouldn't be deterred by our side conversation.

Erika continued to ignore him, though, and her thoughts seemed a million miles away. "I would've gotten away with it, too. I was this close." She pinched her thumb and forefinger together tightly. "But then you had to go and ruin it, Missy. I hope you're happy. Here I did us all a favor and now you want to see me punished for it. That's the only thing that's wrong here."

Lance's voice rose, since he was clearly tired of being ignored. "With these rights in mind, do you wish to speak with me?"

"Sure. Whatever." She finally addressed the policeman. "This is all a dream, anyway. I'm going to wake up any second. Any second now…"

"Sorry to disappoint you," Lance said, "but this is no dream. You're arrested for the murder of Mr. Herbert Solomon."

CHAPTER 23

By the time I slogged back to Crowning Glory after the drama in the lobby behind me, I carried the weight of the world on my shoulders.

Watching Lance escort Erika Daniels to his squad car left me even more drained than I'd expected. Here I'd sped through the day on a massive dose of adrenaline, which had continued through the confrontation in the lobby, but now, slowly but surely, my energy began to flag. At this point, I wanted nothing more than a hot bath and my cool bedsheets.

Beatrice glanced up at me when I schlepped through the doorway of the studio.

"There you are!" Her excitement rattled the chandelier earrings she wore. "People have been calling here nonstop. I was about to send out a search party for you."

"Thanks, but I'm okay." I made my way to the counter and shimmied onto a bar stool.

"Everyone knows about Erika Daniels," she said. "Everyone. It's all anyone's talking about. Can you believe she spent all day working in our studio, and we had no idea she was the murderer!"

"Tell me about it." My gaze wandered to the shiny mirrored tiles behind Beatrice's head. Somehow, the decorations seemed even colder now, and not at all chic, since I knew the person responsible for choosing them. "Do you think we can get our old stuff back? I don't even want to look at this furniture anymore."

"Sure, I don't see why not. The building manager said he'd store our stuff for us until we figured out what to do with it." Beatrice had moved from behind the counter, and she chose the bar stool next to mine. "What happened when Detective LaPorte arrested her?"

"It was crazy. Definitely one for the record books."

I proceeded to tell her everything about the afternoon: from the way Waunzy reacted to the tainted wallpaper, to the way Erika tried to blame *me* for the crime. The tale was so outrageous, Beatrice moved closer and closer to my bar stool, until I could count every sequin in her chunky earrings.

"That's incredible!" She finally leaned away. "She's gone completely off the rails. I'm so glad nothing happened to you."

"Me too. But you know, we've dealt with all kinds of criminals around here. You'd think we'd be used to it by now."

One of the worst crimes involved a murder at the Sweetwater mansion at the start of the new year. The killing was bad enough, but then Ambrose found a bloody cross at the crime scene and that brought the "crazy" to a whole 'nother level.

Then there was the time a killer zeroed in on someone the night before a big wedding at Morningside Plantation. The poor victim ended up on the dirty floor of a public restroom, only steps away from the elegant ballroom where the wedding was supposed to take place. And, finally, what about the lunatic who murdered someone and then stuffed her body in a rain barrel? All those killers had devised unique ways to deal with their enemies, and none of them had accepted responsibility for their actions afterward.

"You should've been there, Bea. Erika denied everything. All of it. Turns out she knew exactly what she was doing when she told Herbert Solomon to use that bedroom."

Beatrice flinched. "That's diabolical. Who could do that to another person?"

"Psychiatrists would say they're narcissistic, but it doesn't matter. The only thing that matters is that Lance has her in custody and Ivy Solomon knows who murdered her husband. That's what counts."

At that moment, the door to the studio swung open, and who should enter the room? Ivy Solomon, as if she'd eavesdropped on our conversation through a hole in the wall.

"There you are!" She immediately headed for the counter, where she proceeded to give me a big hug. "I heard all about what happened to you. You poor thing!"

She wore a different St. John suit today—an understated gray number with pearl buttons—and her face was wild with worry.

"Don't fret about me, Ivy. I'm fine." I pulled away from her to downplay what'd happened. "Really. Lance had everything under control."

"You say that now." She shook her head. "When I think of what that girl could've done to you. *Brrr.* It gives me shivers."

"I'm just glad she's in custody." I still could picture the look on Erika's face when Lance slapped handcuffs around her wrists and led her away from the lobby. "She actually thought she could blame everything on me and Lance would believe her."

"That's what I heard, too," Beatrice said. "Everyone knows she's a lunatic."

Ivy reached for my hand now. "Thank you for going out on a limb like that. I never expected you to put yourself in harm's way for me."

I twined my fingers around hers. "It's the least I could do. But enough about me. How are you holding up?"

While she appeared normal from far away, the minute we stood eye to eye, I noticed that deep circles underscored her eyes and the creases above them had deepened even more. She obviously hadn't slept in days.

"I'll be okay." Her fingers pressed against mine. "At first, I was so angry at Herbert, I didn't have time to be sad. I know this is hard to believe...but I still loved that man, even after everything he did to me."

"You're a saint." I could only imagine her shock when she first found out about her husband's affair, especially since it happened in the very mansion where she'd come to spend her time while she planned his funeral. "If I were you, I would've clobbered Evangeline Roy first and let the cops ask questions later."

"Believe me, I wanted to." She leaned away from me, her fingers still laced around mine. "But then I remembered what you said: She's not worth my time. Why should I drive myself crazy thinking about her, when Herbert and I had some good years together before she ever came along? We're talking twenty good years, and only one bad one."

"Atta girl," I said. "Don't let her ruin that for you."

All this talk about her late husband reminded me of one last question I longed to have answered. "Say, Ivy. I know it's probably too soon to ask you this, but what will you do now?"

She shrugged. "What I've always done. I'll go back home to Baton Rouge and rattle around in my big ol' house. What with Herbert gone, and Trinity, too..."

"Then don't go home," I blurted out. Although I was as surprised as anyone by my response, the idea wasn't so far-fetched. "You own a lot of property down here in Bleu Bayou. Why don't you take over Dogwood Manor and turn it back into a house?"

She quickly shook her head. "No. I don't think I could do that. As a matter of fact, I've been thinking about something. Now, tell me if you think this idea is crazy."

She finally pulled her fingers away from mine, and I replaced my hand in my lap. "Okay. What did you have in mind?"

"I want to donate Dogwood Manor to the city of Bleu Bayou. Just give it away."

It took a moment for her words to sink in. When they did, my face broke out in a grin. "That's wonderful! The city would love to have the property. You could donate it to the Bleu Bayou Historical Society. I know the person who runs it, and she'd treat that mansion like gold."

"Wow." Beatrice spoke so loudly, her earrings once more jostled. "That would be so cool! Maybe the city could turn it into a museum."

"That's what I was thinking," Ivy said. Although haggard, her face looked more peaceful now. "Maybe something good can come from all of this. I was going to call the mayor in the morning and tell him."

"I know he'll accept the offer," I said. "He'd be crazy not to. And then you'd have a good reason to come down and visit me."

"That's the other thing I was thinking." She smiled and turned to leave. "Looks like I'll be coming to your shop a whole lot more in the future."

"Which I'd love." I nodded at Beatrice. "We'd both love it. You can drop in on us any old time. The door is always open."

Ivy waved as she made her way through the studio. Once she reached the French door, she didn't have time to open it, though, because someone else rushed into the studio. It was Ambrose, who ducked around Ivy and made a beeline for the counter.

"There you are! I've been worried sick about you." He threw his arms around me as soon as he reached the counter.

"I'm okay," I squeaked. "Uh, Ambrose? You're kinda suffocating me."

"Sorry." He reluctantly pulled away. "It's just that my imagination got the best of me. I kept thinking about how that horrible woman could have hurt you. What if she took you hostage?"

"Oh, Bo. You've been watching too many cop shows on TV." I managed to smile again, which felt so wonderful after the stress of the past hour. Just knowing Ambrose worried about me meant I finally could relax. "I'm fine. Really."

"So, what now?" Beatrice asked. "What's going to happen to Erika Daniels?"

"Well…" I leaned back on the bar stool, warmed by the feel of Ambrose's hand on my shoulder. "Since Lance has her in custody, she'll be formally charged with first-degree murder. That's because she planned everything to a T. I guess we'll have to testify against her at some point."

"Yuck." Beatrice shuddered. "I don't know whether I can face her, after what she did."

"It's okay, Bea. You don't have to do it alone. We're all in this together."

"Now, where have I heard that before?" Ambrose's tone was playful. "Oh yeah. It was the first time you found a dead body around here. No, wait. I think it was the second."

"Don't tease her, Ambrose." Beatrice shot him a look. "It's not Missy's fault she keeps finding dead bodies. Or that the detective wants her to help him. She's just curious, is all."

"Hmmm. Isn't that what killed the cat?" he asked.

"Stop it." I swatted him, knowing full well it wouldn't make a lick of difference. "Maybe I should just hide out in my workroom from now on, so no one can find me."

"Normally I'd agree with you," Ambrose said. "But I've got a better idea. I know you haven't had a thing to eat today, and I'm starving, too. How about if I take you back home and we both clean up for an early dinner?" He threw Beatrice a glance. "Would you mind?"

"Not at all. I can hold down the fort. I think Missy should take a couple days off, to tell you the truth."

"Would you two stop talking about me as if I wasn't here?" Although I tried to sound peeved, no one was buying it. "I guess I can leave for the rest of the day. It helps that we have the interview with *Today's Bride* behind us."

"Plus, now you don't have to worry about paying Erika for all this stuff." Beatrice waved her hand around the room. "I can work with the building manager to get our things out of storage. Then I'll work on getting everything else cleaned up and returned."

"That'd be great." My shoulders felt lighter and lighter. "It'd be wonderful, actually. I guess it's true what they say about the grass being greener on the other side. I mean, c'mon. Right now, I'd give anything to have our old studio back again."

"It sounds like Beatrice is gonna make that happen, so you're free to have some fun." Ambrose cupped my chin in his hand. "I promise I'll make you forget all about Erika Daniels."

"I don't doubt it." I leaned in for a good, long kiss, until Beatrice cleared her throat.

"Okay, you two lovebirds. Get a room already. Let's keep it G-rated around here."

"That's what Odilia LaPorte always says." I laughed at the coincidence. "I guess it's unanimous."

Ambrose helped me off the stool and deposited me on my feet. "Enough chitchat already. Let's get going before anything else happens."

He winked at Beatrice, who slyly winked back.

Neither of them knew I had witnessed it. "Okay, you two. What's going on?"

Bo pretended not to hear me, while Beatrice suddenly became fascinated by a spot on the counter.

"Really," I said. "What's going on?"

"I don't know what you're talking about." Ambrose began to pull me through the studio, as if he couldn't get me away fast enough. "I'm just taking you out for a nice, well-deserved meal."

He gently nudged me through the French doors, until I landed in the parking lot. I glanced down to avoid the harsh glare of the sun, and that was when I noticed the stains on my white slacks. Although they were clean enough for the interview, sawdust freckled the pant legs now, and carbon powder dirtied the knee. Time to shower and change into a fresh set of clothes.

We hotfooted it across the parking lot, steam rising from the asphalt in waves. Luckily, Ambrose's Audi sat in the second row. I headed for the passenger side, where I hopped from one foot to the next.

He swung open my door with a flourish. "Your carriage, madam."

I dove onto the passenger seat and watched him walk around the hood of the car. He whistled while he walked.

"So, nothing's up?" I asked, when he entered the car from the driver's side. "Since when did you take up whistling?"

"Since today. It seemed like a good time to start."

Since he obviously wasn't going to confess to anything, I gave up trying to pry it out of him. Instead, I watched the scenery pass my window as we drove along LA-18.

Soon, we approached Dippin' Donuts, the bakery owned by Grady Sebestyan. Grady was the former flirtation of mine that had gone horribly awry.

It felt like a lifetime ago, but only eight months had passed since Grady asked me out to dinner. It turned out to be one of the longest nights of my life, since he wouldn't talk about anything but himself and his glory days playing high school football.

Although Ambrose and I weren't even a steady couple at that point, I missed him the entire time. I longed to see his face on the other side of the picnic table at Antoine's Country Kitchen, instead of Grady's.

"Whatcha thinking about?" Bo glanced at me in the rearview mirror as he drove.

"I don't know." We drew nearer to the bakery, where a fluorescent arrow shot from the roof. "Okay, that's not true. I was thinking about my date with Grady."

"Ugh." Bo's gaze promptly returned to LA-18. "Did you have to bring *that* up?"

"Hey...you asked what I was thinking about. It feels strange to see Grady's bakery now. I thought he'd never stop talking about himself that night. Talk about an ego."

"Trust me, I remember." Apparently, Ambrose had bad memories from that night, too.

"The worst part is, I can't go back there now. And Grady makes the best beignets. Guess I'll have to do without."

"Not necessarily. You always could order 'em off the Internet. Heck, I'll even order you a batch from Café Du Monde in New Orleans. That way, you'll never have to see Grady again."

"Really, Bo? We're talking about Bleu Bayou here. I'm bound to run into him at some point."

"Then I'll definitely order you some from Café Du Monde. At least that'll improve your odds."

"Why, Ambrose Jackson. I do believe you're still jealous."

"Of that guy?" Ambrose puffed out his cheeks. "*Pppffftt.* Don't be ridiculous."

While he said one thing, Bo's actions said another. He floored the gas pedal until the car whizzed past the bakery. We didn't slow down until the Sweetwater mansion appeared on the right-hand side of the road.

Here was my excuse to change the subject. "Say, I wonder whether Hank knows what happened this morning?" By now, most people in town should know about Erika Daniels's arrest, thanks to the local rumor mill.

"Hard to say." Ambrose snuck a look at the mansion, too, as we drove past.

Fortunately, Hank remembered to close his front door this time, and the lion door knocker eyed me as we moved down the road. "Remember that night when we found him asleep in his dining room, with the front door wide open?"

"Sure do," Ambrose said. "He helped us polish off a bottle of wine, if I remember correctly."

"That's right," I said. "Waunzy told me Hank wanted to buy Dogwood Manor at one point. Guess he won't have the chance to do that, since Ivy wants to donate it to the city."

"I'm not surprised."

"I think he and Waunzy Boudin should go into business together and find another old house to renovate. She has the know-how and he has the money, so it could work out."

A moment later, the cottage I shared with Ambrose appeared on the horizon, in all its bubblegum-pink glory. In addition to the blush-colored paint, a trellis of yellow crossvine, which I'd planted earlier in the summer, added a splash of color to the wall.

Ambrose pulled the car into our driveway. "Time for a nice dinner, and I'll then research how to buy you beignets off the Internet."

"Thanks, Bo." I opened the door on my own this time and began to amble up the walk. Unlike my earlier, disastrous, date with Grady, I fully intended to spend lots of time on my hair and makeup for my date with Ambrose.

Once inside the house, I headed for my bedroom, which sat at the end of the hall. The closet door stood open, and clothes tumbled onto the pine hardwoods. Several shirts hung half-on and half-off their hangers, and a pile of shoes covered the floor. My stuff seemed to multiply overnight during the wedding season, when I barely had time to breathe, let alone clean out my closet.

I reached for one of the first things I spotted: a tropical Lilly Pulitzer shift, which was my go-to option for special nights. My hand stalled over the hanger, though, since the shift's neighbor offered an intriguing alternative. A pure-white Carolina Herrera dress, with cap sleeves and a neckline embroidered with gold thread, which I'd bought on a whim at a local resale shop.

I chose the Carolina Herrera, then pawed through the pile of shoes until I found some Steve Madden wedges. The cherry-red shoes were a little bold, which somehow felt right after the craziness of the day.

I quickly dressed, then headed to the bathroom to fix my hair and makeup. My bathroom shared a wall with Ambrose's, and the *plink* of water hitting shower tile sounded through the wall.

Interesting. Bo rarely showered in the evening, since he took an extra-long one each morning before work. *I wonder what that means?*

With a shrug, I returned my attention to the mirror. I'd carefully applied makeup before my interview with *Today's Bride*, but that was hours ago. My cheeks looked pale again, and my eyes bare, since the taupe shadow and charcoal eyeliner were long gone.

After washing my face, I brushed more Chanel Rouge blush on my skin. Then I added smoky-gray eyeshadow and ringed my eyes with more liner. I stepped back to appraise the result.

Not bad. Then again, maybe I needed the makeup to detract from my frizzy hair. The humidity always managed to plump my hair up to ridiculous lengths, and my auburn locks looked like an untamed lion's mane.

I took my hairbrush firmly in hand. Once I made up my mind, I brushed everything into a high ponytail, which I secured with an elastic band. Then I wound a few strands of hair around the base of the ponytail, to hide the plastic, tucked in everything nice and tight with a bobby pin, and *voilà!* I had a sleek, simple design, which would complement the clean lines of the dress and my pearl stud earrings.

I flicked off the bathroom light when I finished and sauntered down the hall, renewed by the makeover. Ambrose met me near the front door. He wore my favorite polo, which matched his Tiffany-blue eyes to a T. My heart flip-flopped at the sight of him.

"Awww...you wore my favorite shirt!" I leaned into him and noticed the Acqua Di Gio cologne on his neck. "And my favorite cologne. You are so sweet."

"Me? Look at you. You look like a million bucks. I'm just grateful you let me hang out with you."

He leaned forward to kiss me, and I didn't resist.

After several seconds, I finally pulled away. "Uh, Bo? If we don't get out of here soon, we're never going to make it to the restaurant."

"That wouldn't be so bad, would it?" He gave me another kiss, this one even longer. It was a miracle my knees didn't buckle on the spot.

The only thing that kept me upright was a dull ache that corkscrewed through my stomach. "We have all evening, Bo. But if I don't eat something soon, you're going to have to scrape me off the floor with a spatula."

"Well, we can't have that." He finally released me, then wrapped his arm through mine to escort me through the house and onto the driveway. As always, he gallantly swept open the passenger door when we reached the Audi, then closed it again, once I'd settled onto the seat.

"By the way...where're we going?" I asked, once he had a chance to open the driver's-side door.

"It's a surprise. But it's someplace special. You're going to love it. Promise."

"There you go again...being mysterious. Trust me, I've had enough mystery for one day."

"You can never have too much mystery." He gave a throaty laugh, which made my knees turn to jelly again.

The only way I'd make it through the car ride without pouncing on him was to focus on something other than his handsome face. So I turned to the window and began to study the scenery around me. In no time at all, we'd driven to the outskirts of Bleu Bayou, which meant that dinner at Miss Odilia's Southern Eatery was out of the question. Ditto for the *Riverboat Queen*, a former steamship docked on the banks of the Mississippi.

The highway narrowed as we began to move into the countryside. Soon I spied a petroleum plant with shiny silver tubes that crisscrossed like a child's jungle gym. An orange flame shot from a smokestack on the end, the color translucent in the early evening sky. I closed my eyes when I suddenly remembered the last time I'd seen the plant.

"Uh-oh," I said. "I think I know where we're going."

"You do?" Ambrose sounded disappointed. "And here I wanted to surprise you."

"Don't worry." My eyes fluttered open again, and I placed my hand on his knee. "I'm still surprised."

Sure enough, the rough-wood sign for Antoine's Country Kitchen appeared up ahead. Ambrose took a hard right, and the car careened into the pea-gravel parking lot.

The restaurant in front of us wore sheets of corrugated tin on its roof, raw-wood planks on its porch, and whittled-pine posts that held everything up.

The place looked like a fish-camp bunkhouse, one that would offer crawfish—what the locals called "mudbugs"—any day of the year, and not just during crawfish season in the spring.

Despite its rough exterior, though, critics from New York to Florida loved the place. Even Ruth Lehcier of *Appetites* magazine lauded its down-home menu and authentic atmosphere. That was the word she used…"authentic." While I would call it "kitschy," who was I to argue with one of the country's most famous food writers?

Fortunately, the praise didn't go to the chef's head, and the restaurant continued to get rave reviews from everyone who posted about it on the Internet.

"Are you sure you're surprised?" Ambrose still looked disappointed, those beautiful blue eyes cloudy now. "You're not mad at me for choosing it, are you?"

"Mad?" My heart melted all over again when I saw the look on his face. "No, of course not. I'm glad you brought me here. Seriously. I never had a chance to eat my dinner the last time, since I lost my appetite when Grady started talking."

"Good." He sounded relieved. "I'm glad you have an open mind. Best of all...today's Wednesday. You know what that means, don't you?"

"Zydeco night!" I squealed the response so loudly, folks halfway across the parking lot probably heard me.

"Yep." Ambrose gave me a crooked smile that melted what was left of my heart. "There's no telling what could happen tonight."

CHAPTER 24

Ambrose happily escorted me up the rough-wood planks that led to the front porch. As we climbed, the sound of music leached through the weathered floorboards. It was the *clickety-clack* of a rubboard, keeping time to a wheezy accordion and a hyperactive fiddle.

We entered through the front door and landed in a massive dining hall. The room was dark, or maybe it just seemed that way after the brightness of the parking lot, so I waited for my pupils to adjust to the light, and then I carefully followed Ambrose through the hall.

It looked like a giant warehouse, with exposed ductwork overhead, more two-by-fours on the walls, and acid-washed concrete for the floor.

We skirted a ring of people who moved around a parquet dance floor on our way to a picnic table. Music flowed from a raised stage, where a Cajun band sat beneath a plastic banner that read THE CAJUN COUNTRY STOMP SWAMPERS. Like before, a man in a red vest crooned a Cajun tune with his lips so close to the microphone, they nearly touched it.

"*Hé tite fille, héite Fille tite fille, ooh tite fille…*" he sang, his voice soulful and raw.

I expected to see an old man behind the singer with his rubboard, like before, but a young girl sat there now. She ran a spoon along the rubboard's crimped edges, and the *clack-clack-clack* kept the accordion, fiddle, and steel guitar in check.

"*Où Tas été hier aux soir,*" crooned the singer, oblivious to anything but the music.

Ambrose pointed to an empty table on the outskirts of the dance floor. The minute I settled onto the bench, I pulled a menu from a clothespin attached to the table's edge and began to read the offerings.

"Say, Ambrose." I pretended to study the menu, knowing full well what I wanted to eat. "What would you think if I ordered frogs' legs?" It was a little test, which might've been sneaky, but I really wanted to hear his response.

He cocked his head. "Frogs' legs? That's what you want? Okay, then… go for it."

Bingo. I ducked my head and smiled. With Grady, I never got a chance to make my own decisions; it was always about what *he* wanted. My Ambrose not only listened to me, but he obviously cared about my opinion.

"What's the matter?" he asked. "You just sighed."

"Yeah, but it was a happy sigh. I really want the shrimp étouffée, but I thought I'd ask you about the frogs' legs anyway."

"And you thought I was being weird tonight?" He chuckled and rose from the table. "If you stay here, I'll go place our order."

While Ambrose left to join a line at a nearby counter, I scanned the room. Like before, pictures of famous zydeco musicians—including Buckwheat Zydeco, Dr. John, and Boozoo Chavis—lined the walls. The dance floor took up most of the space—which was nothing new—and picnic tables ringed the periphery like an afterthought.

The room was as kitschy as ever. Too bad I'd never gotten to enjoy it the first time around.

"All set." Ambrose returned to our table and slid onto the bench across from me. "It's nice to see you smiling again."

"Why wouldn't I?" A thought suddenly crossed my mind, and I straightened. "Let's dance."

"Dance?"

"Yes. I'd like to dance. Just until our food gets here."

"I guess so." He shrugged, not the least bit threatened by my change in plans.

I took his hand and practically pulled him to the dance floor, giddy with happiness. The band had launched into a tune that called for the Zydeco Bounce.

The dance steps were simple, really, and we picked them up right away. After moving four steps right, and then four steps left, we shuffled back four steps, dipped forward, and then returned to our original spots.

The second time around, when I took four steps back, I almost collided with the dancer behind me.

"Whoa!" the stranger said.

I turned to see a good-looking man about my age—just north of north—who wore a plaid country-and-western shirt and a black felt cowboy hat. He tipped the hat and smiled. "Watch out there, little lady."

"I'm sorry." My voice was barely noticeable above the music.

"Not me," he said. "Name's Hunter. Hunter Brown."

He extended his hand, oblivious to the people dancing all around us, but Ambrose intercepted the handshake before I could return it.

"Back off there, Hunter." He nudged the man's hand away. "This little lady's already got a date."

"Hey, no problem." The cowboy quickly dropped his hand and shuffled away.

"Let's get out of here," Ambrose said.

By now, the crowd had moved on to the forward dip, and couples bobbled all around us. Ambrose took my hand and led me toward the exit.

I pulled my hand away when we got to the edge of the dance floor. "But what about our food?" There was no telling when it would arrive, and I couldn't imagine eating cold étouffée.

"It's okay," he said. "I'll take care of it later."

I shrugged and followed him to the exit. If he didn't balk when I spontaneously asked him to dance before dinner, then I couldn't balk now.

He threw open the door, and we stepped out onto the porch. By now, the sun had stalled on the horizon, and the orange glow resembled the ethereal flame of the smokestack. It was a beautiful sunset, accompanied by the lilting sound of zydeco music.

Bo nodded to the back of the porch, where we walked.

"What's up, honey?" I asked, once we stood in the corner.

Instead of answering me, he slowly sank to one knee and pulled a box from the pocket of his khakis.

Time slowed. I recognized the light blue box in his hands...and I knew the logo for Tiffany & Co. But, somehow, my brain couldn't process it.

When it finally caught up with the moment, my hand flew to my mouth.

"Missy," he began, his face more serious than I'd ever seen it, "it's no secret how I feel about you."

The musical notes softened as my thoughts flew back to the very first time I had met Ambrose Jackson. It had happened in my new studio, when a shopkeeper arrived from next door to welcome me to the Factory.

He was gorgeous, with chestnut hair, a strong jaw, and eyes the color of robins' eggs. Right then and there, I thanked my lucky stars for bringing him so close to me. But then, as the morning wore on, he'd told me about his late wife, a pretty catalog model who'd lost her battle with breast cancer.

He obviously adored her, because his eyes misted whenever he said her name. Right then and there, I put him in the "friend" category and vowed to give him time to grieve his late wife.

"Missy?"

My hand slowly fell to my side. "Uh, what?"

"I asked you a question, honey."

"You did?"

He laughed. "Yes, and it'd be nice to hear your answer. I just asked you to marry me."

No more thinking was necessary. Just when I opened my mouth, a cell phone blasted a ringtone that shattered the quiet.

Dagnabit! Of all the times for someone to call me...

"Don't worry...I won't answer it." My voice was wispy, since I'd suddenly forgotten how to breathe. "They can leave a message."

"Okay...let me try this again. Missy DuBois, would you marry me?"

He stared at me with those beautiful blue eyes, which sucked the last bit of air from my lungs.

"Oh, Bo. You don't know—"

A second ringtone sounded, this one even louder than the first. Ambrose half-rose from the floor and plucked the phone from his back pocket.

"Let me turn this off." He moved to do just that when his hand stalled. "Uh-oh. It's the police department. You'd better check yours, too."

Numbly, I reached for the phone in the pocket of my dress, wanting nothing more than to smash it on the floor. But, sure enough, Lance's number appeared on the screen.

"Oh, shine." I gazed at him helplessly. "What should we do?"

"Just a second." He straightened completely and tapped the screen. The phone stopped ringing, and then he held it out to me. "He sent us a text, too. They found another body—this one in the bayou. And you'll never believe who it is..."

About the Author

Sandra Bretting has written for several national newspapers, including the *Houston Chronicle* and the *Los Angeles Times*. A graduate of the University of Missouri School of Journalism, she currently lives with her family in Houston, Texas. Readers can visit her website at www.SandraBretting.com.

Printed in the United States
by Baker & Taylor Publisher Services